Why had they gone after her?

Drew's instincts told him to put miles between himself and the men who had pursued him all the way from Europe. But he couldn't leave Melinda unprotected.

He'd been gone for three weeks with the sensor alarms turned off. It was possible his pursuers had breached his security. In a matter of minutes he located a listening device.

They were listening. They'd overheard his conversation with Melinda when she came to his apartment, and they knew she was important to him. Their plan must have been to grab her and use her for leverage to make him do what they wanted.

He would never let that happen. Not to her.

Or to their baby.

CASSIE MILES

INDESTRUCTIBLE

TORONTO • NEW YORK • LONDON
AMSTERDAM • PARIS • SYDNEY • HAMBURG
STOCKHOLM • ATHENS • TOKYO • MILAN • MADRID
PRAGUE • WARSAW • BUDAPEST • AUCKLAND

To the brilliant, imaginative Melissa Jeglinski.
And, as always, to Rick.

Special thanks and acknowledgment to Cassie Miles
for her contribution to the Maximum Men series.

Recycling programs
for this product may
not exist in your area.

ISBN-13: 978-0-373-74514-2

INDESTRUCTIBLE

www.eHarlequin.com

Printed in U.S.A.

ABOUT THE AUTHOR

Though born in Chicago and raised in L.A., Cassie Miles has lived in Colorado long enough to be considered a semi-native. The first home she owned was a log cabin in the mountains overlooking Elk Creek, with a thirty-mile commute to her work at the *Denver Post*.

After raising two daughters and cooking tons of macaroni and cheese for her family, Cassie is trying to be more adventurous in her culinary efforts. Ceviche, anyone? She's discovered that almost anything tastes better with wine. A lot of wine. When she's not plotting Harlequin Intrigue books, Cassie likes to hang out at the Denver Botanical Gardens near her high-rise home.

Books by Cassie Miles

CAST OF CHARACTERS

Drew Kincaid—A freelance reporter who specializes in extreme sports. Unafraid to take any physical risk, he has the ability to self-heal.

Melinda Winston—Swept off her feet by Drew, this quiet librarian at Augustana College finds herself pregnant and thrust into wild adventure.

Dr. Kenneth Sykes—A brilliant but unethical scientist, he developed special abilities in his subjects and seeks to control them.

Blue—An unstoppable thug who works for Sykes.

Lily Timmons—Head librarian at Augustana College.

Pamela Forbes—Drew's former girlfriend, who left him while she was pregnant.

Belle Anderson—Drew's foster mother until he was eighteen, she's a cold, distant woman.

Harlan Anderson—Drew's foster father kept dark secrets of his own and lived a double life.

Claudia Reynolds—A computer whiz who has dedicated herself to stopping Sykes and helping her lover, Jack.

Jack Maddox—His special ability is precognition, and he's determined to find his twin brother, who is still being held captive by Sykes.

Chapter One

For as long as he could remember, Drew Kincaid knew he was different. Some people called him crazy. Some said he was the luckiest man on the planet. And there were those who wanted to lock him up and throw away the key.

Since the day he turned eighteen, he'd been on the run from a faceless, nameless enemy. Today, ten years later, his luck might have run out.

Before dawn, he slipped through the back door of the rustic, seaside hotel outside Naples, Italy. Making his way toward the south end of town, he hid in the shadows on narrow streets. Light shone through some of the windows; the fishermen awakened early.

Behind a stucco house with a painted orange door, he found the bicycle he'd stashed yesterday. He would have preferred an Italian, carbon-frame racing bike like the ones used for the Giro d'Italia, but this three-speed was serviceable. It would do.

His tires hummed on the cobblestone road. As he rode toward the edge of town, he heard the pitched barking of a dog, the cries of gulls, the slamming of a car door. Glancing over his shoulder, he saw no one on the road behind him.

Within a half hour, he was in open countryside, climbing a steep, curving road that led to the cliffs overlooking the Mediterranean. He pedaled hard, sweating under his thermal windbreaker. His backpack held only the essentials: a change of clothes, bottled water and his laptop. He kept his flash drive, passport and cell phone in his pockets.

His stories for this assignment had already been filed electronically with *World Sport Magazine,* the New York–based publication that financed this three-week trip to Europe to cover the extreme skiing competition in the Alps and the bicycle marathons in Spain and Italy—an incredible range of sports, considering that it was only March.

Drew wasn't employed by *World Sport.* Though he remained doggedly freelance, he sure as hell wasn't opposed to taking an assignment like this one. An expenses-paid trip to Europe? An insider's pass to interview elite athletes? A chance to try his hand at extreme skiing? Oh, yeah, he loved his work.

A week ago in Verbier—a ski resort in the Swiss Alps—he noticed that he was being followed. In spite of his evasive maneuvers, they'd been coming closer. Drew needed to get back to Sioux Falls. When he came face-to-face with these guys, he wanted home field advantage.

The problem was getting out of Europe in one piece. He arranged to meet up with a Cessna pilot in Sorrento. From there, they'd fly to Rome, where Drew would make his connections back to the States.

At a high point on the Amalfi cliffs, he pulled onto the shoulder. This seemed like a good place for cell phone reception, and he wanted to check with his pilot. Standing beside a cypress tree at the edge of a forty-foot precipice, he looked down at the sea. White froth roiled and rushed against the jagged rocks below him. In the opposite direction, the sun was rising over Mount Vesuvius.

There was a text message from Melinda Winston.

As soon as he saw her name, he grinned. Though Drew never had a place he considered home, being with Melinda gave him a warm, cozy, comfortable feeling. He liked almost everything about her—from the way her auburn curls fell softly past her shoulders to the slender curve of her waist to her delicate ankles and pink toes. She was always quick to laugh at his jokes, and he never had the sense that she was playing games or trying to manipulate him. There was nothing phony about her. A librarian, she was a solid, Midwestern woman with solid, Midwestern values. Except when they made love. He'd been lucky to find her, living in the apartment directly under his.

Her text said, "Home on Wed? Dinner at my place?"

His first impulse was to call her back so he could hear her voice, but the time difference meant it would be the middle of the night where she was. He texted: "I'm there. Six p.m."

He almost added the word *love,* but it wouldn't be right. As soon as he returned to Sioux Falls, South Dakota, he needed to move. Now that his enemies knew his identity, they'd be coming after him. His dinner with Melinda might be the last time he saw her. Regret tugged at his heart. If his life hadn't been so damned crazy, there might have been a chance for something more between them.

He called the pilot and verified that he'd be there within half an hour.

Back on the bike, he rode steadily on the cliff-side road. Thoughts of Melinda occupied his mind. He'd bought her a present while he was in Switzerland—a souvenir to remember him by when he left her.

He heard the engine of a car behind him, turned his head to look. A black sedan. Coming right at him. He veered off the road. The car followed.

Nowhere to go. They were too close. This bike wasn't made for off-road maneuvers.

The car aimed directly at him. Abandoning the bike, he ran through the shrubs and grasses that separated him from the brink of the steep, white cliff.

Car doors slammed. He heard yelling. Two voices. Two of them and one of him.

No time for finesse.

Running as hard and fast as he could, he leaped over the edge. For a moment, he flew. His arms churned, grabbing at the air, fighting for distance. He hoped to jump wide of the rocks at the base of the cliff. He almost made it.

Feet first, he landed on a sharp outcropping. His left leg crumbled, and he sprawled. His left arm jolted. His hands scraped against the jagged stone. Pain shot through him.

Still, he managed to push himself into the sea. The temperate Mediterranean waters were cold against his overheated body. He swam underwater as far as he could.

When his head broke the surface, he saw two men standing on the cliff. Even at this distance, he recognized something familiar about the shorter man with white hair. The other had a shaved head. He was holding binoculars.

Drew dove under the water again. His left leg was virtually useless, but he managed to get beyond a spit of land, out of sight from the cliff. He climbed onto the rocks.

Ignoring the pain, he inspected the injury to his leg. The bone wasn't visibly broken, but there was already swelling around his ankle. His hands looked worse, as thick blood oozed from the abrasions. The little finger on his left hand bent at a weird angle.

He closed his eyes and concentrated, listening to the steady, strong beat of his heart. Injuries never stopped him.

As a kid, he'd been quick to heal. As he got older, he learned to focus the healing. His body needed little direction or encouragement. His blood surged toward his injuries. His muscles repaired themselves at a cellular level. His torn flesh knitted.

In a matter of minutes, he was healed.

His head throbbed from the strain. Later, he'd need a long nap. Exhaustion and a headache were the downside to his miraculous talent—the ability that made him a freak.

MELINDA WINSTON stared at the big, round, old-fashioned clock that hung on the kitchen wall in her one-bedroom apartment. In slow motion, the second hand ticked down. Four minutes and forty-five seconds until six o'clock.

She knew that Drew was home from his travels; she'd heard him climbing the stairs to the third-floor apartment just above hers. Though he'd texted an acceptance to her dinner invitation, she halfway expected him to call and cancel. Any normal person would need a rest after a three-week assignment in Europe. As if Drew Kincaid was normal? Not hardly!

His job as a freelance reporter for sporting events had to be the most fantastic occupation she could imagine. On a moment's notice, he'd be on a plane to Aspen or Hawaii or Alaska. She'd never even heard of some of the extreme sports he covered; most of them weren't available on basic cable. All of which made it rather bizarre that he chose Sioux Falls as his home base. Even more strange was the fact that he was living here in a plain, old, three-story brick apartment building not far from the Augustana College campus where she worked in the library. Most preposterous of all? They were dating.

Why would an exciting, handsome, incredible man like Drew be interested in her? Not that she suffered from low self-esteem, not much anyway. But Melinda faced facts. She wasn't stylish, gorgeous or even athletic. From the first time he'd kissed her, she'd told herself that this relationship wouldn't last. When they'd fallen into bed together after watching an evening performance by the Augustana Madrigal Choir, she allowed herself to be swept away by fierce passions unlike anything she'd experienced in her twenty-six years. He'd made her feel like a truly exotic creature, elevated far above the realm of dull reality. Golly darn, it was amazing. She'd felt beautiful and remarkable, capable of conquering the world, climbing Mount Everest, racing a Ferrari.

When the afterglow had faded, she'd put on her glasses and looked in the mirror. Other than her thick, curly, light auburn hair, which was definitely her best feature, she considered herself to be pretty much average. Her mouth was too big, but her teeth were straight and white. Drew said that when she laughed, it looked as if she was taking a bite out of life. A very tactful compliment because she tended to snort when she really got to chuckling.

Nobody in their right mind would confuse her with a fashionista jet-setter. She'd never even been to Manhattan, much less Paris or Madrid. Her only major travel came when she was in junior high and made it to the finals of the National Spelling Bee in Washington, D.C., where she'd bombed out in the third round after misspelling *cataclysm.*

The wall clock ticked down to one minute and fifteen seconds. Hoping to quiet the excited thumping of her heart, she inhaled a deep breath and smelled the aromas of roast beef, mashed rutabaga and a freshly baked apple pie. She never attempted fancy cuisine when she cooked for Drew. He'd tasted the real thing.

She centered the silver candlesticks that had once belonged to her grandmother on the small round table in the dining area adjacent to the kitchen. Was this the atmosphere she wanted? Candlelit romance? Probably not. She had important news for Drew. She took the candlesticks back to their place of honor on her knickknack shelves.

Maybe she could wait to tell him after they'd made love. *Just one more time.* It was possible that she'd misjudged his probable reaction. He might be happy. He might surprise her and—

She heard his knock on the door and ran to open it. He looked even better than she remembered. The light from an antique-looking sconce in the wainscoted hallway picked out sunny highlights in his light brown hair. His complexion was tanned from being outdoors, and his deep-set green eyes shone with a warm, sexy light. Though he was wearing a simple black sweater and jeans, he had an air of casual elegance and absolute confidence.

He held out a bottle of wine. "I'd like to say that I bought this in Naples, but it's from the duty-free shop at JFK."

"That's fancy enough for me."

When he entered her apartment, the plain white walls and bland Scandinavian furniture seemed special and dramatic. The glow of his personal charisma lit up her boring bookshelves, making her collection of mysteries and spy thrillers look like esoteric tomes.

He set down the wine bottle on the table, caught hold of her hand and gave a tug. Offering zero resistance, she flowed into his embrace. Her body fit perfectly with his. She was a little over average height at five feet nine inches, but he stood over six feet and easily dominated her. Her head tilted back, welcoming his kiss. When his lips pressed firmly against hers, her internal temperature shot up to a thousand degrees. Her blood was hotter than molten lava.

No one had ever affected her like this. She hated to think of what her life would be like without him.

He ended the kiss with a gentle caress that slid down her back and finished with a light swat on her bottom.

"I brought you a present," he said. "Direct from Switzerland."

"You didn't have to."

"I didn't have wrapping paper." He reached into his back pocket and held up a wristwatch. "There was a bit of an accident. It got wet but seems to be working okay."

She held the watch in her hand. A plain beige leather band and a silvery face with the red Swiss cross as a logo. "It's beautiful. And practical."

"Like you."

"I think I'll take that as a compliment."

"It was this or a Swiss Army knife. I liked the watch better."

She peeled off her old watch, replaced it with his gift and held up her wrist. "I'll never be tardy again."

He sniffed the air. "Do I smell pot roast?"

"And potatoes and buttery rutabaga. We can start with a salad."

"I'd rather start with the meat."

Not surprising. Drew was definitely a carnivore. He trailed her into the kitchen, opened the drawer beside the sink and found the corkscrew. It pleased her that he knew his way around her apartment.

"Tell me about Switzerland," she said.

"I was covering competitions in extreme skiing. Off-piste is what they call it. These skiers go way out of bounds on glacier ridges with sheer vertical drops. I gave it a try on a snowboard and almost got caught in an avalanche."

"Geez Louise, Drew." She gaped. "Why would you take that kind of risk? Why would anybody?"

"For the rush." He pulled the cork out of the wine. "And the views are pretty damn spectacular. Nothing but snow and sky and mountains. In Zermatt, I could see the Matterhorn."

"I'd be just as happy to look at a postcard," she said as she served up the salad.

"That's because you haven't tried the real thing. There's a thrill that comes from challenging yourself, pushing the limits."

While she set the salad plates on the table, he went back into the kitchen. She watched as he reached up to the top shelf in her cabinet for the wineglasses. His broad shoulders tapered to a lean torso and a tight butt. Talk about a spectacular view!

"The way you live," she said, "it's like you're on a continuous roller coaster. I'm more of a carousel person."

He poured two glasses and handed one to her. His head cocked to one side as he studied her. "There's something different about you. New hairstyle?"

She shrugged. "Nope."

"Your glasses," he said. "You aren't wearing your glasses."

She reached up to adjust the frames that weren't there. "I guess I'm not. That's odd. My vision seems okay without them."

"I like it." He clinked his wineglass against hers. "Let's drink to your eyes."

As soon as the glass touched her lips, she remembered. She shouldn't be drinking. She lowered the glass.

"What's wrong?" he asked.

She could have made up an excuse, but she'd never been good at lying. Her lips pinched together. She didn't want to tell him. Not yet. "Golly, I just don't—"

"Come on, Melinda. Take a sip. Are you afraid that you'll get drunk and lose control?"

"Don't tease." She wasn't in the mood for banter.

"I promise not to ravish you until after dinner. Have some duty-free wine."

"I can't," she blurted. "I'm pregnant."

The look on his face was one of sheer panic.

Chapter Two

Drew drained his wineglass in one gulp. He made his living with words, describing athletic feats with precision and flair, but he couldn't think of a damned thing to say.

His plan for tonight had been to see Melinda one last time before he faced the impending threat to his life. He had no choice but to leave her. If he stayed, she'd be in danger.

He hadn't wanted their goodbye to be final. Someday, she could be part of his life. But not now. Not while she was carrying his child.

"Are you…" His voice strangled in his throat. "Are you…sure?"

"I've taken five pregnancy tests. The result is always positive."

"But you haven't been to the doctor."

"I'm sure," she said angrily. "My periods are as regular as this Swiss watch you gave me. When you left on your assignment, I was a week late.

Ten more days after that, I faced facts, peed on a stick and voila!"

Dumbfounded, he couldn't help but stare at her stomach. "How did this happen?"

"Good question. I'm on the pill, and it's supposed to be ninety-nine percent effective."

For a moment, he considered that his seed was as invulnerable as the rest of him. But that couldn't be. He'd been to bed with plenty of women who hadn't turned up pregnant. It had only happened once before. "But I used condoms."

"Except for that one time," she said. "There's no point in second-guessing what we should have done or who was at fault. Spilt milk, you know. No use in crying over it. And it's pretty clear how you feel about this."

"Give me a minute. I'm not sure how I feel."

"I'd like for you to leave."

He gazed down at her delicate face. The beautiful eyes he'd toasted only a moment ago flared with righteous anger. He couldn't blame her; he wasn't handling this well. "I'm not going to abandon you. Whatever you decide is—"

"Spare me the phony nobility, okay? I'm going to have the baby, and I have no intention of roping you into support payments or anything else."

He started to object, to tell her that he wasn't

the kind of man who cut and run. But that was exactly his plan: to leave her until there was no possibility of danger, which might take a long time. Hell, it might never happen. "Let me explain."

"No explanation necessary. I told you about my pregnancy because it was the right thing to do. You deserve to know. That's the end of it." She went to the door and held it open. "Please go."

Hostility crackled around her in a ring of fire. Still, he reached toward her, hoping to connect. "I'm glad you told me."

"Don't touch me." She had never looked so beautiful, so powerful. "At least show me the respect of doing as I ask."

As soon as he stepped into the hallway, the door slammed with absolute finality. Slowly, he trudged up the wooden staircase to his third-floor apartment, fitted the key in the lock and went inside. The halogen lamp on his desk shone down on his battered laptop, which probably wasn't going to survive immersion in the Mediterranean—the dunking that had taken place when he was being chased by dangerous men who wanted to do him harm. How the hell could he explain that to Melinda? How could he tell her that he was a superhealing machine, and a dark, faceless enemy was after him? He never shared his secrets. If anyone else knew, they might also be targeted. No way could he drag Melinda into the maelstrom of his life.

Stretched out on the leather sofa, he stared up at the high ceiling with the old-fashioned, frosted glass fixture. He'd chosen this old, brick apartment building because of the prewar charm and the fact that the landlord was willing to issue his lease to one of Drew's fake identities. None of his mail came here; it was delivered to a P.O. box in Manhattan. He paid his bills online. This apartment was untraceable—a safe haven where he could hide while he dug into his past and found out what had happened to him when he was growing up in South Dakota.

And that was exactly what he should continue to do: find the answers. He should take Melinda's advice. *Leave her alone. Let her have her own life*.

As a rule, he kept his relationships short-term and uncommitted. He hadn't expected to get involved with Melinda, hadn't expected to care so much about her.

But he did care. He wanted her in his life. And their baby. *My God, I'm going to be a daddy*.

An incurable ache squeezed his heart. He'd suffered a lot of injuries in his life, but losing Melinda and his unborn child was a scar that his miraculous, regenerative blood couldn't heal.

MELINDA GLARED angrily at the ceiling. As far as she was concerned, Drew Kincaid could go straight to hell. She'd never forget the look of terror on his face when she told him. What happened to the daredevil who skied down an avalanche? Was he scared of a baby?

Apparently, yes.

She needed to burn off some of this anger. Though it was chilly and dark outside, she'd go for a run. In the bedroom, she peeled off her clothes, threw on her sweats and jammed her feet into well-worn running shoes.

Before she left, she decided to put away the dinner she'd prepared for him so she wouldn't have to face it when she came home.

She picked up the unused china from the table. Her mother had given her the delicate Wedgewood blue-patterned plates for her hope chest. They were supposed to be for after she got married. That wasn't likely to happen now. Melinda was seven months away from becoming a single mother.

This wasn't the way her life was supposed to work out, but she wasn't totally miserable about the prospect. She wanted children, and she had to admit—though she was furious at Drew—that he was an excellent sperm donor: healthy enough to tackle all those extreme sports he seemed to love.

Smart enough to be a decent reporter. Motivated enough to make a success of his life. *I could have done worse.*

A heavy sigh pushed through her lips. Drew's flaw was his inability to make a commitment. A man like him didn't want to be tied down, and it wasn't as if he'd made her any promises.

Neither of them had ever declared their love. *Do I love him?* The word had been poised at the tip of her tongue once or twice. But she hadn't actually said it.

With the plates put away, she surveyed the massive dinner. All this food would go to waste; she didn't have the appetite to sit down and eat.

But Drew probably did. He must be starving and wouldn't have food in his house after being away for three weeks.

On a paper plate, she put together helpings of pot roast and rutabagas. Might as well give him the entire apple pie. Being pregnant meant she ought to concentrate on healthy foods that would nourish the baby. And, of course, she should return his wine.

With both hands full, she climbed the stairs to his apartment, intending to place the food outside his door then return to her apartment, call and tell him dinner was served.

As she approached his door, it opened.

She held out the plates. "You might as well have this food. I'm not hungry."

He took her by the arm and pulled her forward. "We need to talk."

"Be careful. I don't want to spill." She allowed herself to be led into his apartment, where she set down the plate, the pie and the wine on the kitchen counter. "I invited you for dinner. And here it is."

He closed the door to his apartment, folded his arms across his broad chest and leaned against the door. "A long time ago, I made myself a promise. If I was ever so blessed as to become a father, my child would have a better life than I did in foster care."

She didn't know he'd been raised in foster care. Drew never spoke of his childhood, and she'd assumed that he came from a privileged background. With all his jetting around the globe, he seemed like a trust-funder. "What happened to your birth parents?"

"They're dead. I have no family."

He spoke with such harsh finality that she couldn't bear to look at him. Her gaze darted around the room. Though Drew had lived here for almost four months, his apartment still looked unsettled. There was a desk, a huge leather sofa with a coffee table in front of it, a television, two straight-back chairs and not much else. No pictures on the walls. His reference books and magazines were stacked around his desk in piles.

"Melinda, I want to do the right thing."

"Don't worry. I would never cut you out of your child's life."

"*Our* child," he said. "This baby belongs to both of us."

This simple, obvious declaration sank deep into her consciousness. No matter what she did for the rest of her life, she'd be connected to Drew through their child. "Why do I feel like I should apologize? I didn't get pregnant by myself, you know."

"I haven't forgotten one minute of our love-making."

Neither had she. When he took a step toward her, she retreated. "You just stay over there."

"That's not what you really want. Tell me how you're feeling, Melinda."

"I'm confused." She felt an incongruous smile sneak onto her face. "And I'm excited. I love babies, and I've always wanted children. Single motherhood is a difficult prospect, but I know my parents will be supportive. They always are."

"How do you feel about us?"

"Well, I can't help wishing things were different."

"I'm not good with relationships," he admitted.

"Ooooh, big surprise."

"Sarcasm? That's the coward's way out."

"I don't know how I feel about you because I don't know you." When they talked, he told her about his adventures and the exotic places he'd been. She knew nothing about who he really was. "I didn't even know you were a foster kid."

"You want a biography? Fine. I bounced around in foster care until I was ten. Then I was placed with Belle and Harlan Anderson in Lead. That's a little town in the Black Hills near Rapid City. I was a loner, but I had a girlfriend in high school. My first love. She died in a car accident."

Though the tone of his voice remained steady, she heard an echo of sorrow. "I'm sorry."

"On my eighteenth birthday, I went to New York. It's a good place to disappear, and that's what I did. I was too busy trying to survive to make friends. I managed to get to my senior year in journalism school while working a regular job and an unpaid internship at a sports magazine. I fell in love."

Melinda was glad to know these sketchy details about his past. Even if Drew wasn't destined to be part of her life, their child should know something about his father. "What happened with that relationship?"

"She left me."

As he moved toward her, she could see the tension

in the set of his jaw. When he talked about his first love, he'd been almost wistful. Now, he was angry.

"There's more to that story," she said.

"Her name was Pamela Forbes. She got a job offer in Europe and didn't want to settle down."

He stood directly in front of her. The magnetism she always felt when she was close to him arced between them, but she resisted. She hadn't come upstairs to fall into bed with him.

She wanted to understand him. If there was a possibility of a relationship, she didn't want to close that door. She owed it to herself and to her unborn child to figure out what role Drew would play in both their lives.

"Sounds like you were furious with Pamela."

He shrugged, trying to dispel his tension. "What was it you said? Spilt milk? There's no point in looking backward."

"You can learn a whole lot from past mistakes."

"I found out that Pamela was pregnant. She wasn't honest like you, didn't step up and tell me. But I found out. And when I heard, I was happy. I saw a chance for a normal life. Married with children. It was too much to hope for."

Gosh, he was cynical. Why shouldn't he expect a normal life? Instead of understanding him better, she was even more confused.

He continued, "I bought a diamond ring in a

pawn shop and went down on one knee to propose. That's when she told me she'd been dating other men, her company was sending her to Paris and she'd already made an appointment for an abortion. I never saw her again."

"You haven't had much luck with commitments." She was beginning to understand why he'd gone into shock when she told him about the baby.

"As long as I'm being honest," he said, "I was going to tell you tonight that I'm leaving Sioux Falls. It's necessary for me to be out of touch for a while."

"What does that mean? Out of touch?"

"I won't be able to communicate with you."

"Wait a minute." Before she came upstairs to his apartment, she'd been adjusting to the idea that Drew wouldn't be in her life. But this was too abrupt. "Wherever you go, there are going to be phones."

"As soon as possible, I'll contact you. Until then, is there anything you need? Is your insurance in order? Do you need money for a doctor?"

"I don't believe this." A raging fury exploded behind her eyes. "You're trying to buy me off."

"That's not what I meant."

"You expect to write me a check, pat me on the butt and send me on my way." She dodged around him and made a beeline for the door. "No, thanks. I don't need or want your money."

She stormed into the hall, raced down the stairs to her apartment and slammed the door. The nerve of him! Sure, he'd had a rough life and bad luck with relationships, but that didn't excuse the way he'd treated her.

She paced furiously. To the bedroom. Back to the front room. Into the kitchen. Her apartment was too small to contain her anger. *How dare he offer me money!* She stamped her running shoe on the hardwood floor. *Who in the blazes did he think he was?*

When she heard the knock on her door, she figured it was Drew again. "Go away. I don't want to see your face."

Another knock. More insistent.

She flung open the door. Before she could speak or react, a bright flash of light blinded her. Then everything went dark.

She crumpled to the floor.

Chapter Three

Standing over the sink, Drew jabbed a spoon into the center of the apple pie and dug out a bite, hoping that the sugar rush would help him feel less like an ass.

The pie tasted great. Sweet, tart apples perfectly complemented by a flaky crust that crumbled on his tongue. Homemade, of course. Probably a recipe passed down from her dear old granny. Melinda's family tree went back for generations. No way should she be involved with a rootless loner like him.

He shoveled in another bite of pie.

From downstairs, he heard a crash. Apparently, Melinda hadn't gone for a run even though she'd been dressed for jogging in her smooth black pants with a white stripe and matching sweatshirt. There was another loud thud. It sounded like she was tearing apart her apartment, throwing things, breaking furniture. *Terrific.*

He'd managed to drive a completely rational woman to the brink of madness.

He saw two options: he could close his ears, pretend nothing was wrong, leave in the morning and never look back. Or he could stand and fight for her. Damn it, he wanted Melinda in his life. He needed to make her understand that he had enemies and there was a very real threat. Unfortunately, that meant he'd have to tell her the whole truth.

Not yet. More pie.

He licked the back of the spoon and listened. The sudden quiet from downstairs felt ominous, like a vacuum had sucked the air from her apartment. Was she sitting in the dark, cursing him under her breath? Did she own a gun?

He wiped his mouth with a paper towel and headed for the door. Moving fast so he wouldn't change his mind, he went down the staircase.

When he knocked on her door, it pushed open. She'd left it slightly ajar. "Melinda?"

He stepped inside. An end table lay on its side. Books scattered across the floor. Her sofa had been shoved out of place. Her apartment had been trashed.

This can't be. He didn't want to believe the evidence that lay before him. Someone had been here. *His enemies had gone after her.*

Cold night air blasted through the window that opened onto the fire escape. He rushed toward the long, beige curtains that were flapping in the breeze and peered down at the asphalt parking lot behind the building. A vehicle pulled away from a spot beside the Dumpster. A dark sedan.

Had they taken her?

Desperately, he called out, "Melinda, where are you?"

The sound of a whimper drew him toward the arched hallway. She was in the bathroom, sprawled beside the claw-foot tub. A thick smear of red blood marked the black-and-white tiled floor.

As she propped herself up on her arms, she winced in pain. Her zippered sweatshirt had been torn off. From the waist up, she wore only a gray sports bra. There were welts on her arms. She was still bleeding from a puncture on the inside of her elbow.

He knelt beside her, gathered her into his arms. He had to get her away from here before they came back.

She looked up at him. Her pupils were dilated. "Drew?"

"I'm here," he whispered. "Do you think you can stand up?"

"How did I get into the bathroom? What happened?"

"Don't you remember?"

"I opened the door." She licked her lips. "And there was a flash. A blinding light."

He'd seen that flash. Hundreds of times when he was growing up. There was a burst of light, and he'd black out. Sometimes, he'd be awake within an hour. Other times, it was days. "I have to get you to safety."

Gamely, she struggled to stand up. Her legs were unable to support her weight. She collapsed against him. "What's wrong with me?"

He checked the darkening bruise on the inside of her arm at the vein and made an educated guess. "I'd say you've lost some blood."

"I need a doctor."

"Come with me." He needed to get her away from here before they came back.

Leaning heavily against him, she stumbled into her living room. "What happened in here? Was I robbed?"

Explanations were going to take a while—time they didn't have. He lifted her off her feet and carried her toward the door, where he came face-to-face with a uniformed policeman holding a gun.

"Freeze," the officer ordered.

Standing behind him was Melinda's neighbor from across the hall—a gray-haired woman who taught anthropology at Augustana. "It's all right," she said to the policeman. "He lives in the building."

"Put her down on the sofa." The cop's gun didn't waver. "Do it now."

Though Drew knew he was capable of disarming the cop, he did as ordered. It was never wise to assault an officer.

The professor rushed to Melinda's side. "Are you okay?"

She nodded slowly.

The neighbor smoothed Melinda's hair off her forehead. "I heard crashing and peeked into the hall. Your door was partly open, and I saw a man inside. I called the police."

"Can you describe the man?" Drew asked.

"I didn't get a good look." The professor's cheeks were flushed. Beneath her gray bangs, her forehead furrowed. "He was Caucasian. Definitely mesomorphic."

"What's that?" the cop asked.

"Large, muscular body structure," she said. "And he had a shaved head."

Any doubt Drew might have had about the identity of the intruder vanished. Melinda's attacker was the same man who had been after him in Italy.

LESS THAN AN HOUR later, Melinda walked through the door of the health services clinic at the college with Drew at her side. He'd insisted on driving and now hovered close to her.

"Are you sure you want to go here?" he asked.

"I hate hospital emergency rooms." The shock of being attacked in her own home made her want to seek the safe and familiar. "I know the people here."

Physically, she didn't feel too terribly bad. Her injuries had been far worse after a Rollerblade accident. But the memory loss was worrisome. It didn't seem like her head had been injured. What else could cause a blackout?

Holding her arm, he directed her into the room. Slate-blue chairs lined the walls in the small waiting area, and two students huddled in the corner. Both were coughing and sniffling. The woman in pink scrubs who sat behind the counter looked up from the book she was reading. Melinda recognized her; she was a frequent patron of the library.

"Melinda," the nurse said. "What happened?"

Drew answered for her. "She was assaulted. We need to see the doctor right away."

His intensity must have impressed the nurse because she quickly escorted them to a small room with an examination table and the typical medical paraphernalia arrayed on a countertop beside a sink. She turned to Drew and said, "You can wait outside."

"I'm staying here."

The nurse helped Melinda onto the table. "You're in luck, hon. Dr. Lynn is on duty tonight until nine, and she's the best."

"Thanks, Ruth." Her recall of the nurse's name was somewhat reassuring. Her long-term memory seemed to be unaffected by the assault. Only the few moments after the flash remained blank. "You didn't really have to rush us in here. It looks like other people were waiting."

"No problem." She patted Melinda's hand. "You sit tight, hon. You're going to be okay."

When she left, Drew came closer again. "Do you want to lie down? Should I get you some water?"

"Give me some space, okay?"

He backed off one pace. "How's this?"

"That extra eight inches is really swell." He didn't take his eyes off her for a second. She couldn't help but comment on his change in attitude. "I thought you were in a big hurry to leave town."

"Not anymore," he said. "I'm staying with you."

"What if I don't want you around?"

"You'll get used to having a bodyguard."

A bit overprotective, but she liked being taken care of. The attack upset her. That kind of violence wasn't supposed to happen to people like her. She'd always lived a very quiet, very safe, very average life.

Doctor Bethany Lynn entered. In spite of her horn-rimmed glasses and blond hair pulled back in a severe bun, she looked like a teenager. Melinda knew that Doctor Lynn was in her late twenties and she liked to read Jane Austen.

After the doctor introduced herself to Drew and shook his hand, she focused on Melinda. "Tell me what happened."

"I wish I could. I was alone in my apartment. I opened the door and got hit by a bright flash of light. After that my mind is blank until Drew came into the bathroom and found me lying on the floor."

The doctor shot a vaguely suspicious glance toward Drew. "Why did you go to her apartment?"

"I'm Melinda's upstairs neighbor. I heard crashing."

"And the woman who lives across the hall from me also heard the noises and called the police. She saw a strange man inside my apartment."

"Was it a burglary?" the doctor asked. "Was anything taken?"

"Not even my purse," Melinda said. "The police think Drew scared him off before he could take anything."

"Take off your sweatshirt, and I'll get started." Dr. Lynn continued to ask simple questions while she examined Melinda's bruises, paying particular attention to the wound on the inside of her arm. "This is on the vein. Was there a lot of blood?"

"Just a few smears," Melinda said.

She wrapped a cuff around the uninjured arm to test blood pressure. "Any vomiting?"

"No."

"Ringing in the ears? Dizziness?"

"I'm really tired. Kind of weak in the knees."

The doctor ran through a couple more tests. "Your blood pressure is a little low, and you're slightly anemic. The bruising appears to be superficial. Mostly defensive."

"What does that mean?"

"Your arm was grabbed with force, and you were dragged. While you were trying to fight off your attacker, you bumped into things, which caused the crashing noises." The doctor gave her a reassuring smile. "I'd like to ask some personal questions. It might be best if we were alone."

"I'm not leaving," Drew said. When he folded his arms across his chest, it looked like they'd need a bulldozer to remove him from the examination room.

"It's okay with me if he stays," Melinda said.

Dr. Lynn didn't look pleased, but she continued, "Were you sexually molested?"

"Golly, no." If she'd been raped, Melinda would have felt it. "I still had my pants on."

"I was downstairs pretty quickly," Drew said. "Five or six minutes after I heard the first crash."

Ignoring him, the doctor examined Melinda's eyes. "You don't appear to have a concussion, but your amnesia concerns me. I'd suggest you go to the hospital for a CAT scan."

"I'm pretty sure I don't have a head injury. What else would cause a blackout?"

"You might have been drugged. I should take a blood sample and run tests to find out."

She hadn't wanted to acknowledge that possibility. "Drugs might be a problem. I'm pregnant."

Behind her glasses, the doctor's eyes widened. Of course, she'd be surprised. She knew Melinda was single. "Well, congratulations."

"Thank you," Drew said.

His fierce protectiveness was softened by a proud smile. If he'd given her that kind of warmth when she first told him, she would have been elated.

Not anymore. She was leery of Drew.

After they left the clinic, her suspicions deepened when he drove past the turn leading to their apartment building. "Where are we going?"

"Not home," he said. "That's for damn sure."

Exhaustion crept over her. Too tired to argue, she leaned back in the passenger seat and groaned. "I need to go to sleep. In my own bed."

"You can sleep in the car. I have a cabin that isn't too far from here."

"Absolutely not." She mustered just enough strength to resist his ridiculous idea. "Tomorrow I have work."

"Being assaulted qualifies you for a sick day."

Taking time off wasn't a problem in terms of her employment, but she was concerned about the people she worked with. "If I don't show up at the library tomorrow, everybody is going to worry. They'll be calling to make sure I'm all right and bringing over casseroles. I don't want to cause a fuss."

And how would she explain that she was running off to a secluded cabin with Drew? She'd mentioned to Heather and Lily Rhoades, the head librarian, that she was dating, but that was a far cry from spending a weekend at his cabin. Or being pregnant with his child.

This was all too much. She groaned again. "Please just take me home."

After checking the rearview mirror, he pulled over to the side of the road and parked his SUV. He turned to her and took her hand. "I know a little something about danger. We can't go back. It's not safe."

She had the terrible feeling that he might be right.

Chapter Four

"Take me home," Melinda said. "Or I'll scream."

If Drew could have forcibly abducted her, he would have done so. The danger was right here, in her face, undeniable. She'd been assaulted in her own home.

"Be reasonable, Melinda. We have to get out of here before they come back."

"They?"

"You're in danger."

"You're making too much of this," she said. "Like the policeman said, this was an attempted robbery. I'm not surprised. There's really no security in our apartment building. The lock on the front door opens right up if you shake it hard enough."

"This wasn't a run-of-the-mill robbery. He dragged you into the bathroom and drew blood."

"We can't be sure that happened."

A streetlight outside the window shone on her cheekbone and jaw. Her quiet beauty disarmed him, and he felt guilty for sucking her into the peril he'd lived with for most of his life.

He couldn't expect this very normal woman to grasp what it was like to live on the razor's edge, and he didn't know how to explain without sounding like a lunatic.

His truth wasn't easy. He'd have to break it to her gently. "At least, let me take you a hotel tonight."

"Oh, gosh, no. I can't let you go to all that trouble and expense. I'm fine, Drew. The best thing we can do is leave the investigating to the police and get on with our lives."

"It's not just your safety," he said. "You have to think about the baby."

She rubbed at her forehead. "I'm getting a headache."

"You can't close your eyes and pretend this didn't happen. Nobody likes to think they're in peril, but—"

"You do," she said. "You go looking for danger. Extreme danger."

"That's my job."

"And I'm a librarian. That's my job, and I want to go to work tomorrow. That's final."

"Are you always this stubborn?"

"With most people, I'm the very soul of coop-eration. You bring out the worst in me." She yanked down on the door handle and swung it open. "If you won't take me home, I'll walk."

"Close the door."

"We're going home?"

"Fine."

Maybe she was right. He'd taken precautions. In case of this very situation, his apartment was set up like a fortress.

On the short drive back to their building, Drew kept an eye on the rearview mirror, making sure they weren't being followed. The streets of Sioux Falls, bathed in moonlight, were as quiet and serene as a Norman Rockwell painting. He told himself that they'd be safe for tonight.

When he parked in the lot near the entrance, he flipped open his glove compartment and took out his .32 Beretta Tomcat—an efficient and accurate pocket-size handgun.

She gaped. "That gun better not be loaded."

As if he'd carry an unloaded weapon? "The man who attacked you wasn't playing games. We need to take precautions."

"Like what?"

"Like going to my cabin."

She shook her head and winced. The doctor had inspected her scalp for head wounds and found nothing, but she seemed to be in pain. "I'm not going anywhere."

"Then stay close beside me. Do exactly as I tell you. We're going to my apartment first."

They managed to get inside the building and up the stairs without incident. Coming here wasn't the best option, but Drew felt relatively safe in his one-bedroom apartment. He'd armed the place like a fortress with three locks on the door, bulletproof glass on the windows and surveillance cameras. After he prowled down the hall and looked into the closets to make sure they were alone, he set his Beretta down on the coffee table. There were three other guns hidden around his apartment.

Melinda had collapsed onto the sofa with her eyes closed. The lamplight shimmered on the strands of gold in her long, curly auburn hair. Utterly peaceful and untroubled, she didn't look like someone who had been violently attacked less than two hours ago.

When he attempted to lift her so he could carry her to bed, she pushed him away. After a huge yawn, she asked, "What are you doing?"

"Taking you to bed."

"I've got a headache." Her lips spread in a sleepy grin. "I never expected to hear myself say that to you. Going to bed with you is, well, it's…" She yawned again. "It's amazing."

Though he hadn't been thinking of sex, her suggestion aroused him. Making love to her had been his number one priority tonight. This evening should have been a "welcome home" celebration—a home-cooked meal followed by hours of mind-blowing passion.

"I want you to sleep here tonight," he said. "In my bed."

"Oh, I hate to be a bother." She pulled a frown. "I'm fine right here on the sofa."

Enough politeness! He tucked one arm under her knees and wrapped the other around her back. With a quick jerk, he lifted her off the sofa. "Whether you like it or not, you're going to be comfortable tonight."

In her pale greenish eyes, he saw a battle between exhaustion and stubbornness. "But I—"

"Hush, Melinda." He gave her a little kiss on the tip of her nose. "Let me take care of you."

With a sigh, she relaxed and nuzzled against his neck. "I'm too tired to say no."

He carried her down the short hallway to his bedroom and settled her against the pillows. By the time he pulled off her running shoes, took off her sweatshirt and tucked her under the down comforter, she was asleep.

Though sorely tempted to join her in bed and hold her against him, Drew had to figure out what to do next.

He went to the kitchen and poured a glass of the

wine she'd returned without drinking a drop. In the living room, he perched on the edge of the sofa and turned on the flat-screen television. Using the remote, he tuned to the channel that displayed the view from three strategically placed surveillance cameras. One showed the hallway outside his apartment. Another focused on the building's entrance from the parking lot. The third camera looked down from the roof and showed the fire escape outside his window. Nothing was moving. Not even a squirrel in the trees.

His instincts told him to put miles between himself and the men who had pursued him all the way from Europe. But he couldn't leave her unprotected. He swirled the wine in his glass and took a sip. Why had they gone after her?

He shoved off the sofa and went to the closet by the front door. Behind the suitcase he always kept ready for a quick escape was a rifle that he'd placed by the door for easy access. On the top shelf, he found a case filled with electronic equipment, including a bug sweeper.

He'd been gone for three weeks with the sensor alarms turned off. It was possible his pursuers had breached his security. In a matter of minutes, he located a listening device attached to the frame of the window that opened onto the fire escape.

They were listening. They'd overheard his conversation with Melinda when she came to his apartment, and they knew she was important to him. Their plan must have been to grab her and use her for leverage to make him do what they wanted.

He wouldn't let that happen. Not to her. Or to their baby.

THE NEXT MORNING, Melinda awoke with the uneasy sense of a nightmare that had already faded into the back of her mind. She opened her eyes. Where was she? Not at home, that much was obvious. Though the layout of the bedroom matched hers, none of her things were here. No knickknacks on the dresser. No family photos hung on the wall.

This bedroom was Spartan and plain. Drew's apartment. He stretched out beside her on the king-size bed, lying on his back. The comforter covered him from the waist down. His chest was bare.

Her gaze lingered. The sight of him was certainly enough to change a nightmare into a dream. His body was long and lean. Not overly muscle-bound, he was built for speed. A sprinkling of hair on his chest arrowed down his torso. His right arm curled above his head. In repose, he looked younger than his twenty-eight years. More innocent. Less troubled.

She reached toward him, trying to remember why she was mad at him. *Oh, yeah, he wanted to dump me as soon as I mentioned the baby.* But he had kind of apologized. And he'd stuck with her last night.

As soon as her hand touched his cheek, he exploded awake. Launching himself off the bed into a crouch, he snatched a gun off the bedside table and aimed at the bedroom door. His green eyes glittered. He was one hundred percent alert.

"Light sleeper?" she asked.

Without a word, he strode from the bedroom into the hallway. His snug black undershorts outlined his tight butt. She would have appreciated the view a whole lot more if he hadn't been stalking.

In spite of his insistence that they flee the city and hide out in a cabin, she didn't really believe they were in desperate peril. Last night's robbery was nothing more than a random event. And she felt much better this morning.

Her headache was gone, thank goodness. As she propped herself up on the pillows, she didn't feel achy or sore at all. *Nothing to worry about.* She was going to be all right.

Drew returned to the bedroom and sat on the bed beside her. "How are you feeling?"

"Surprisingly good."

He reached for her arm. "Let's take a look at that bruise."

When he peeled off the bandage, the dark black-and-blue area inside her arm had faded back to an almost normal skin color. How could that be? Automatically, she reached for her glasses, then remembered that she hadn't been wearing them, didn't need them. Vaguely, she remembered hearing that a woman's vision improved when she was pregnant. She'd always thought that was an old wives' tale. But maybe not.

Drew leaned down and kissed the spot on her arm that had been injured. "Looks good."

"I can't believe I'm better already. Guess I wasn't hurt that badly."

"Yeah," he said, "I'm a fast healer myself."

Waking up together, even if they hadn't made love last night, felt sweet, and she was tempted to carry their easy intimacy to the next level with a kiss. Would it be so bad to make love to him one more time? The answer, unfortunately, was yes.

If she let her guard down, she'd only be hurt. There was no way they could be together. He had his globe-trotting profession. She had her cozy lifestyle. And never the twain would meet. She cleared her throat. "I don't suppose you have coffee."

"I didn't, but I took the liberty of raiding your apartment last night and taking your coffee. It's brewing. I also grabbed some bread and butter for toast." He paused. "And I packed a suitcase with things I thought you'd need."

"Why?"

"We can't stay here, Melinda. Last night, I found a bug outside the window."

She was pretty sure that he wasn't talking about an insect. "A listening device? Like in the spy novels?"

"My enemies overheard us talking last night. They know you're important to me, and they want to use you to get to me."

"Let's do a reality check." She pulled her arm from his grasp and hiked up the comforter to cover her sports bra. "We're in Sioux Falls, South Dakota. In a plain, old apartment building. I'm a librarian, for pity's sake. Nothing exotic ever happens to a person like me."

"Brace yourself." He rose from the bed. "Get dressed and meet me in the kitchen. I owe you an explanation."

In his bathroom, she found the toiletries she generally used in the morning. He'd packed her bags? He wanted to whisk her away to his secret cabin?

She splashed water on her face and brushed her teeth. When she first hooked up with Drew, she knew he was too good to be true. Handsome, smart and funny. Now she knew the downside. He was nuts, delusional. *Or was he?* Was his job as a globe-trotting journalist a cover for a more dangerous occupation?

She put on her zippered sweatshirt and went to the front room, where he sat on the sofa drinking coffee from a Sioux Falls souvenir mug. "If you're a spy," she said, "who do you work for?"

"I'm freelance." He leaned back on the sofa, and his bathrobe gaped open, showing a sexy glimpse of chest hair. "You know that."

"You're not CIA? Not part of some mysterious undercover network?"

"I'm not a spy." He rose and went toward the bathroom. "Help yourself to coffee. I'll be back in a minute."

When he left the room, she glanced around. Her baby blue suitcase on the end of the sofa was the only bright touch in an otherwise unadorned, masculine room. The window shades were still drawn. A rifle leaned against the wall by the front door. There was some kind of electronic equipment on the table, along with night goggles. On the television, she saw three inset pictures that seemed to be from cameras monitoring the hallway and the outside of the building. *Where was she? The bat cave?*

On the kitchen counter by the coffeemaker was

his Beretta. She poured coffee and made two pieces of toast.

What if Drew's paranoia had some basis in fact? Last night had been scary. That was for sure. She'd never been attacked before. If she could have remembered what happened, she undoubtedly would have been more freaked out. During her struggle, her apartment was trashed. It must have been violent. But was it purposeful? Had Drew's "enemy" targeted her? Why? It just didn't make sense.

When the toast popped up, she slathered on the butter. Thus far, Melinda hadn't had a moment of morning sickness. Her mom said that she'd never been sick while pregnant, and she'd delivered four babies, all girls with Melinda being the eldest. Her baby would be the first grandchild.

As she finished off her toast and washed it down with coffee, she found herself hoping that Drew's paranoia wasn't an inherited trait that might be passed on.

He came into the kitchen and snagged the second piece of toast before she could claim it.

"Hey," she protested. "I made that for me."

"Fine. I wanted pie, anyway."

She'd forgotten about the apple pie. Not exactly a healthy breakfast, but it did contain fruit. "I'll have some of that."

They dished up pie and settled on the sofa since he didn't have a dining table. With her fork, she pointed to the three pictures on the television screen. "Is all this security really necessary?"

"Yes," he said firmly. "And it's also entertaining. See that? On the camera that shows the parking lot? It's the anthropology professor who lives across the hall from you."

"Her name is Katherine Bidwell." Melinda watched the spry elderly woman whose gray hair was pulled back in a tight bun. Bustling to her car, she juggled a plastic water bottle and a satchel of books. "Some people say she's a genius."

"She was smart enough to call 911 last night."

He'd gotten dressed while he was in the bedroom. In his white T-shirt, worn jeans and running shoes, he looked sane and normal. But he was still cuckoo. The evidence was all around. Her packed suitcase. The guns. The surveillance equipment.

She finished off her pie and considered licking the plate, but decided she was full. Leaning back on the sofa, she studied his classically handsome profile. "You said it was smart for Professor Bidwell to call the police. Why can't you do the same thing? Tell the police about your enemies."

"They'd never believe me."

"So you know that your story sounds a little bit, um, crazy."

"But true."

If he really wanted her to run away with him to a cabin in the woods, he needed to give her a far more thorough explanation. "Convince me."

"It all started when I was ten years old. A couple of months after I moved in with Belle and Harlan Anderson…"

Chapter Five

Never before had Drew told anyone about what happened to him while he was growing up. As a rule, he avoided close relationships, a lesson he'd learned as a foster kid. *If you don't have friends, you won't be hurt.*

But now there was Melinda. And a baby. He had to prove to her that he was trustworthy, and that meant telling the truth.

"At the Andersons' house, I was the only kid." Before that, he'd been in group situations. "I had my own bedroom. A place where I could close the door and be by myself."

"Did you like being alone?" she asked.

Though he was capable of spinning a convincing lie to make himself sound like Johnny Normal, he stuck to the truth. "I was pretty much a loner."

An encouraging smile lit her face, and he decided that she was especially pretty in the morning. "Tell me about this room of your own."

"The privacy was exactly what I wanted. I had secrets."

"Like what?"

"Even when I was ten, I liked writing." He composed pages and pages of dorky poetry about trees and sky and the parents he barely remembered and how they'd come back one day. "I had to hide my poems and my beat-up copy of *The Little Prince*."

"I love that book," she said. "Why would you hide it?"

"It's okay for a girl to like a book like that. But a guy? No way. With my own room, I didn't have to be so careful."

Still, he kept his book and the spiral notebook filled with his scribbles hidden behind a drawer in his kneehole desk. He didn't trust the Andersons. The rumor was that they'd lost their own children, three boys. If so, they never told him about it, never talked about themselves and they never showed him family photos.

Sometimes, he caught Belle looking at him with a strange longing in her eyes. Mostly, she was cold. Sparing in her conversation, she regulated his day with terse commands. *Get up. Supper. Bedtime*.

Harlan was a better companion, but his job as a salesman meant he was on the road a lot. On weekends, they'd watch sports on TV. Drew started memorizing baseball stats, and Harlan would test him. That was when his interest in sports started.

"It was an okay setup. I had food, clean clothes and a roof over my head. The house was on the outskirts of town, next to a forest. I'd pack a sandwich for lunch and spend the whole day tromping through the trees." He remembered long afternoons when he lay on his back and stared up at the peaceful clouds as they rolled across the sky.

"All in all, life was pretty good, until a Saturday near the end of May. I woke up and got dressed. The next thing I remember was the sun going down while I walked back to the house. The entire day was a blank."

"You had amnesia?"

"I don't want to put a label on what happened." *Not yet, anyway.* "It was like the daylight hours got erased. I wasn't hurt so I didn't say anything about it. Pushed the whole incident out of my head and didn't think about it until it happened again during summer vacation. That time, it was two days."

"Did you tell your foster parents?"

"Yeah." The look on Belle's face was sheer disgust. For a minute, he thought she was going to throw him out, and he didn't want to leave. He liked his private bedroom and watching baseball with Harlan. "They didn't believe me. Told me I was there at home and ate dinner, just like I always did."

Her forehead wrinkled with concern. "You should have seen a doctor."

"Harlan took me to a specialist in Rapid City. The guy ran tests and told me that I had a form of epilepsy that caused blackouts. He gave me pills."

"Did that help?"

"The blackouts stopped. Harlan warned me not to tell anyone about my illness. If the foster care people found out, they'd send me away to a hospital."

In one of her few lengthy conversations, Belle had described the horrors of a place she referred to as the "asylum." She made it sound like a dungeon where he'd be locked up in a cage. The authorities couldn't let crazy people like Drew run around loose. He might hurt someone.

So he kept his mouth shut. "When I was fifteen, the blackouts came more frequently. Sometimes, they'd last for a day. Sometimes, just for a couple of hours. Since I never knew when they'd happen, I missed a couple of practice sessions for the football team. Rather than explaining, I dropped out."

"What position did you play?"

"Running back, and I was pretty damn good. But team sports weren't for me. I started skateboarding, running, riding my bike off-road." He cast a sidelong glance in her direction. "Are you with me so far?"

She nodded. "Everything you've said makes sense, and I'm glad to know about the epilepsy. It's something to watch for in the baby."

"Don't bother. I've had tests run. I'm not epileptic."

She left the sofa and went to the kitchen for another cup of coffee. "What caused the blackouts?"

"I don't know." With his own cup in hand, he followed her. "One of the reasons I moved back to South Dakota was to do research. I hoped to find answers."

"What have you found out?"

"Not much." It was frustrating as hell. He was a journalist—not necessarily an investigative whiz but he knew how to fact-find. "There's no rational way to explain what happened to me. Or the results."

"Results?"

"My physical abilities. Or disabilities. I'm not sure which word applies."

"Stop." She held up her palm like a crossing guard.

He froze with the coffeepot in one hand and his mug in the other. "What?"

"Disabilities? I'm pretty well acquainted with your physical attributes, and I've never noticed anything wrong with you."

"Maybe you haven't explored thoroughly."

"Oh, but I have." She looked him up and down. "I've been all over your personal terrain, from the top of your head to, um, all the other parts."

He placed his full coffee mug on the counter. "I like what you do to all my parts."

She gave him a reluctant smile. "Ditto."

"Your terrain is a lot more interesting than mine." He slid his hands down her torso. "All these nice curves." He reached behind to squeeze her butt. "And this round, firm, sexy bottom."

She subtly shifted position, arching toward him. Her chin lifted, and he knew she wanted to respond to his caresses with the sensuality that was an integral part of her nature.

"You're distracting me," she said.

"That's the idea."

He didn't know how to tell the rest of his story. His theory, developed over the years, was that he'd been experimented on during those blackouts. Whatever they'd done to him changed his blood and gave him the regenerative capabilities that allowed him to heal in a matter of minutes. If he announced to her that he was, in a way, invincible, she'd run like hell. And he wouldn't blame her for thinking he was some kind of nut-job.

Lacking the words to explain, he did what came

naturally. A light kiss. The taste of apple pie sweetened her lips.

He whispered, "Have I mentioned that I'm crazy about you?"

"*Crazy* being the operative word." She used both hands to push him away, then stepped back and leaned against the counter. "Are you going to tell me about this physical thing you have?"

The most obvious way to prove his case would be to take a butcher knife from the drawer by the sink and cut a vein. He could show her his ability. But self-healing took a toll. Today, for their escape, he needed to have all his faculties intact.

"Come away with me, Melinda."

"Don't change the subject." She shook her head, and her auburn curls flopped across her forehead. "You're not going to leave me with a cliff-hanger. What caused your blackouts? Do you still have them?"

"They went away after I left the Andersons' house when I was eighteen." He had timed his escape for the moment when he aged out of the foster system. He was an adult. No one would be searching for him.

"So, you have a clean bill of health," she said. "No serious illness or injury."

"Nothing serious."

She seemed relieved, and he knew her concern

wasn't about him or his health. She was worried about the tiny life growing inside her womb. One of her hands rested on her belly as if she could shelter the baby from harm.

He had the same instinct. Protective. Paternal. He had to keep them all safe. He came toward her, rested his palm on top of hers. "We need time alone, Melinda. To talk."

"You could be right about that."

As he looked down into her greenish-gray eyes, he saw her attitude change. She was no longer wary.

When he was doing interviews with athletes who generally weren't anywhere as articulate as Melinda, he learned to recognize the pivotal moment when they were ready to open up. *That's what he saw in her.* She was coming around to his way of thinking. She didn't want facts; she needed an emotional reason to believe in him.

"Last night, when you told me about the baby, I didn't know how to handle it. I ran. That's what I've always done." He closed the distance between them to a matter of inches. "But I want this time to be different. I want to talk, to plan our future."

"*Our* future? Together?"

Was it possible? Could he settle down and build a normal life with her? Daring to hope, he kissed her.

As their lips joined, he felt her resistance fade.

Her slim, supple body molded to his and her arms encircled him. Her lips parted, and he eagerly deepened the kiss with his tongue.

A sensual energy spread through him. With every beat of his heart, his blood rushed. Holding her felt so right, so good. They'd made love often enough that he knew where she liked to be touched and vice versa. She trailed her fingernails down his back, and the teasing pressure aroused him.

He pulled her tight, wanting to feel her heartbeat synchronized with his, wanting to be a part of her, joined. Was it safe to make love to her now? Could he allow himself to let down his guard? *Probably not.*

He loosened his grasp. Though he'd disposed of the bug, his enemies were nearby and ready to attack, waiting for an opportunity to strike.

He nuzzled her earlobe and whispered, "You're going to like my cabin. It's secluded."

She pulled away from him. "I need to make a few phone calls first."

Though the urge to make love to her was nearly irresistible, his number one priority was to get her to a safe location. "Make the calls on your cell. Let's go. Right now."

Though Melinda really didn't understand his need to hurry, she changed quickly into a well-worn pair of jeans, a blue cotton sweater and a burgundy winter jacket. The weather in Sioux Falls had been pleasantly warm, but there might be snow at his cabin in the Black Hills.

When she turned on her cell phone, there were half a dozen messages. One was from Ruth, the nurse at the clinic. How odd! Surely, it was too early for any results on her blood tests. And the call-back number was Ruth's personal phone.

Drew had already stowed her suitcase in the car. He hovered beside her. "Ready?"

"One minute. I want to return this call."

She ignored the impatient grumbling noises he made. The way she figured, he had no room to complain. He was lucky that she'd agreed to this trip at all. That whole story about his blackouts when he was a kid didn't mesh with his current paranoid state. Just because he had a lousy childhood, it didn't mean people were chasing him.

But she wanted this time alone with him to talk about the baby. Even if she raised the child alone, Drew was still the father.

He took a position near the door, arms folded across his chest. Though she couldn't see the gun hidden under his black leather jacket, she knew he was armed. He looked dangerous and very, very sexy. Which was the other reason she wanted to run away with him. Crazy or not, Drew was hot.

She called Ruth's number. Her message had said "as soon as possible," so Melinda didn't worry that it might be too early for someone who worked the evening shift.

Ruth answered quickly. "I was hoping I'd catch you last night."

"Why? What's wrong?"

"Something happened at the clinic." Her tone was high-pitched and excited. "We got robbed."

"Oh, golly." Never before had Melinda been involved in a violent crime. Then, last night, she was attacked. And she'd just missed being at the clinic during a robbery. What was going on here? "Ruth, are you all right?"

"Thanks for asking, hon. I'm fine. And so is Dr. Lynn. This is the second robbery this year, so we know what to do."

"Why would anybody rob the clinic?"

"People think we keep drugs lying around here, even though we don't have anything stronger than aspirin."

"Then what happened?"

"There was a guy in a ski mask with a gun. He ordered me and the doctor to go into one of the exam rooms and lie on the floor. If we moved, he said he'd shoot. You better believe that I didn't twitch a muscle."

"That seems like the smart thing to do."

"I know." Ruth chuckled under her breath. "You know how much I like to read crime novels, and they always tell you to cooperate if you're being robbed. Drug addicts don't really want to shoot anybody, you know. This guy went wild. He tore the whole place apart."

"What did he look like?"

"I wish I could tell you, hon. After all those mystery books I've read, you'd think I'd be a good witness. But he had on the mask, and I was too busy staring at the gun to notice much of anything else."

Melinda remembered Dr. Bidwell's description of a mesomorphic body structure. "Was he big? Burly?"

"Tall. Not real heavyset. Anyway, that's not why I called you, hon."

"What do you need?"

"Well, this drug addict destroyed all of the samples we were sending to be processed, including the blood we took from you. Dr. Lynn said if we could get you to come back last night, we could take another sample. It might be too late, now. If there were drugs in your system, they've probably worked their way through. How are you feeling this morning?"

"Perfect," Melinda said as she rubbed the healed spot on her arm. "No aches, no pains, nothing."

"Well, if you're still concerned, you could go to the hospital for tests. The clinic is closed today."

"Thanks, Ruth."

After she disconnected the call, Melinda made an uneasy connection between the man who attacked her and the robbery at the clinic. In both cases, blood was involved. Her attacker seemed to have drawn blood from her vein. And her blood sample was destroyed at the clinic. Why the interest in her blood? Was she being targeted by vampires?

"Tell me," Drew said.

"There was a robbery at the clinic. Nobody hurt, but a lot of damage. My blood sample was destroyed."

"Was it the same guy?"

She frowned, wishing she could say for certain. "Ruth didn't get a good look at him. What's going on, Drew?"

"These two events aren't a coincidence. We need to get away from here. Now."

Paranoid or not, she agreed.

Chapter Six

Riding in the passenger seat of Drew's SUV, Melinda tried to connect with her natural optimism. Her cozy life had taken on an aura of danger, and she didn't like the way it felt.

Her gaze stuck on a bald man waiting at the bus stop. Her attacker? Was he carrying a gun in his briefcase? She shook her head. *Stop being so suspicious.* This was a gorgeous, sunlit morning, and nothing bad had happened. Not yet, anyway.

When Drew pulled up at a stoplight, she noticed the shoots of crocuses and dahlias in a corner garden—lovely, green harbingers of spring. Dahlias were poisonous, but not if you didn't eat them—an apt metaphor for her situation. Running away with Drew had definite appeal, but she had to remember: *don't eat the dahlias*.

She'd just gotten off the phone with Lily, her supervisor at the Augustana library, who was shocked to hear about her intruder and happy to give Melinda as much time off as she needed. There was only one little thing…

Bracing herself, Melinda looked toward Drew. "If you don't mind, I need to stop by the library before we leave town."

"We're not running errands."

"Just one stop. There's a project I've been working on, and I should explain it to someone so they can—"

"What part of 'running for your life' don't you understand?"

"None of it," she said. "The closest I've come to being in danger was last night when somebody ransacked my apartment. And I don't even remember what happened."

He slid a cool, green-eyed gaze in her direction. "It's not safe to stop. I circled the block twice and haven't spotted anybody following us, but that doesn't mean they aren't close."

"Or maybe we aren't being followed because there's nobody after us." She really, really, really wanted to believe that nothing was wrong. "Take a left at the corner, go down a block and we'll be at the library. It's next to Ole."

"Ole?"

"The Viking statue." The squat, stone statue with horned helmet, full beard and sword was the college mascot. "He's supposed to be good luck, like a happy little troll."

"I thought trolls were ogres."

"If you're mean to them, they'll get even. But they're lucky for good people." She pointed. "Here's the corner."

Without turning, he cruised through the green light. Apparently, they wouldn't be stopping. She peered over her shoulder, watching as they drove away from the campus. "Don't I get a vote?"

"Not until I know we're safe. It's going to take more than luck from Ole the Viking to get away without a hitch. But don't worry. I've been planning this escape ever since I moved to Sioux Falls. I've got every contingency covered."

Again with the paranoid craziness? "What kind of contingency? Give me an example."

"This morning before we left, I checked the car for bugs and made sure there was no way we could be tracked on GPS. By the way, that means turning off your cell phone."

Her fingers closed around her cell. No way would she give up this link to normal people. "Did you find anything? Any bugs or tracking thingies?"

"No," he admitted.

"Could you possibly be overreacting?"

"No."

He wasn't leaving any room for discussion. "Pete's sake, Drew. It feels like you're abducting me against my will."

"You agreed to come," he reminded her.

"And if I hadn't?"

"I would have thrown you over my shoulder and dragged you kicking and screaming out of the apartment."

Though he grinned, she wasn't altogether sure that he was kidding. She settled back in the comfortable leather seat. By definition, an SUV was supposed to be sporty, but this customized vehicle had a smooth, luxury ride.

They seemed to be headed toward the park, where the falls cascaded in a rush of white water. "Are we taking the interstate?"

"Too obvious," he said. "We'll use back roads. I've got the route all figured out."

A motorcycle pulled into the lane beside her. His engine roared. The rider's helmet was black with three lightning bolts.

Drew looked past her toward the motorcycle, and he reacted. With a swift crank of the steering wheel, he whipped an illegal left turn. *In front of an oncoming bus*.

She covered her eyes and hunched her shoulders, preparing for the devastating impact.

They weren't hit. They made it.

"Why did you do that?" she yelled.

"I didn't like that motorcycle." He checked his mirrors. "But he doesn't seem to be following."

"We could have been killed."

"I knew how much time I had. And the angle I had to take."

"Timing? Angles?" He was crazy. She was being abducted by a crazy man. "How could you know?"

"I cover extreme sports," he reminded her. "That includes motoring events. I've driven in a Grand Prix."

Needing air, she buzzed down the window and inhaled. Over the rumble of traffic, she thought she could hear the falls. Drew took another turn, then another. His route through town was more complicated than her grandma's cable banded knitting pattern—twisting and purling and doubling back. A ten-minute drive took twice as long. And there was nothing Melinda could do to speed him up. He was in charge.

She redialed the number for Lily at the library. "It's me, Melinda."

"What a coincidence! I was just going to call you," Lily said. "There's a man here who wanted to see you."

Melinda looked toward Drew and said, "There's a man at the library, looking for me."

"Get a description and name," he said.

Into the phone, Melinda said, "What's he look like?"

"He's mature, probably in his late fifties. Looks like one of the professors, but I've never seen him before." Lily Rhoades was single and in her forties; she took note of all possibly dateable men. "He's nicely dressed in a sports jacket and jeans. Average height. His hair is graying at the temples."

Definitely not the bald attacker. "Did he give his name?"

"No, but I could ask."

Melinda heard shuffling noises and imagined Lily leaving her desk behind the checkout counter. Then, the head librarian said, "That's odd. He's gone."

"Very odd." Melinda didn't know whether she should be relieved or nervous. If this graying-at-the-temples gentleman was one of Drew's enemies, they'd dodged a bullet by not going back to the library.

"I hear car noises," Lily said. "You're not at home."

"I'm going away for a few days to recuperate." Today was Thursday, and she had the weekend off. "I'm pretty sure I won't be back until Monday at the earliest."

"No problem," Lily said. "You've got plenty of sick time accumulated. Where are you headed?"

"A friend's cabin."

"Mmm-hmm." Lily packed a wealth of innuendo into those hummed syllables. "Would this friend happen to be that guy in your building? The hot reporter guy?"

"That's right."

"Oh, Melinda, that's so romantic. He's going to nurse you back to health."

Their getaway would have been a lot more seductive if Drew hadn't been dodging through traffic. Or if he hadn't swept the car for bugs. Or if he wasn't planning to dump her. "The reason I called," she said, "was that I can't stop in to help out with the project."

"We'll figure it out," Lily said. "You have a wonderful time and get better."

When Melinda ended the call, she turned off her cell phone as Drew had instructed. She loved this little red cell phone and PDA. Not only did it contain all her important phone numbers, but it also included her appointments and notes. Nevertheless, she was willing to chuck it out the window if it brought danger closer to them. "I've heard that you can track GPS through cell phones, even when they're turned off."

"You're starting to believe me," he said.

"A little."

"The GPS in your phone isn't activated unless you turn it on," he said. "I fixed it while you were sleeping."

"Of course you did." He thought of everything. She tucked the cell phone into her purse.

"Tell me about the man at the library," he said.

"It wasn't baldy." She repeated Lily's description. "And I don't think he came across as threatening because Lily sounded like she wouldn't mind going out with him."

"Could be the guy who ransacked the clinic," he said.

She hadn't forgotten about that incident and the danger it brought to Ruth and the doctor. If Drew's reasoning was correct, that robbery was about her blood sample. And the stranger who showed up at the library was after them, too.

"These people," she said. "Once we're gone, they won't hurt anybody else, will they?"

"Doubtful," he said. "The only reason they're after you is because they were listening on the bug they planted in my apartment. They know you're important to me."

"Am I?" Had he changed his mind since last night? When she told him she was pregnant, he'd been ready to run.

"You're carrying my child," he said.

But did he care about her? Without love, there could be no future for them. At least, not a future together.

FOLLOWING THE back-road route he'd mapped out ahead of time, Drew allowed himself to relax as he drove. Across miles and miles of farmland, there had been no sign of pursuit on the mostly two-lane roads. Unless they were being tracked by airplane, he figured they had eluded capture.

The most dangerous leg of their journey was approaching. The Missouri River bisected the state, and he'd chosen the town of Pierre for their crossing. He'd always liked this area, where the Great Plains transformed into the rolling landscape that led to the Black Hills. Once, when he was thirteen, his foster dad had taken him to Lake Sharpe, near Pierre, for a water-skiing vacation.

He glanced over at Melinda. For most of the drive, she'd been quiet and preoccupied. Though he couldn't blame her for being tense, he missed her usual cheerful banter.

"About those friendly trolls," he said. "Are there any you can call on for good luck?"

"Helga." As she spoke the name, a smile touched her lips.

"Your own personal troll?"

"Helga belonged to my grandma. She kept

dozens of little trolls around her house, hiding on the bookshelves and behind the cookie jar in the kitchen. Most were figurines, so ugly that they were cute. Helga was two feet tall and stood by the coatrack at the front door. It was her job to scare off any bad luck that tried to enter."

"I take it your grandmother was Scandinavian."

"Swedish. That's my mom's side of the family. I didn't get the blond hair, but I'm tallish."

"You're tall?"

"Five feet nine inches. That's fairly tall," she said defensively. "You don't notice because I almost always wear flats."

"And why is that?"

"I dress for comfort," she said. "There's no need for me to be fashionable."

He liked her style. A woman who was natural and comfortable with herself was sexier than one who tried too hard. "There must have been a lot of Scandinavians where you grew up in Minnesota."

"I can't believe it. You remember where I'm from?"

"Near Duluth," he said. "I can hear the Minnesota accent in your voice and the way you phrase things. I've never heard you curse. Is that a Minnesota thing?"

"Not really," she said. "I try to be even-tempered, even with people like you."

He took his eyes off the road to really look at her. With her hair tucked up in a ponytail and her legs crossed and her hands folded on her lap, she gave the appearance of a prim, disapproving librarian. He had to look deeper to see the temptress. There was something wild about the way tendrils of hair escaped her ponytail and curled at her cheeks. Her mouth was wide and luscious. Under her practical clothes, her body was a perfect combination of slender and strong.

"Stop staring," she said.

"Do I make you nervous?"

"Yeah, you betcha." She gave an emphatic nod. "You're so…cryptic. You still haven't given me a decent explanation of why these scary people are after you."

If they were captured, she'd be better off not knowing too much about his self-healing ability. "When we get to the cabin, I'll tell you everything."

"How much farther?"

"Pierre is about halfway." They'd already entered the city limits. Traffic was heavier. The possibility of having his enemies find them was greater. "Tell me about Helga."

"Carved from pine and varnished. Helga got pretty scratched up over the years. She had on a dirndl-type dress. Her hair was parted in the middle, and there was a worn spot on the top of her head where we patted her for luck. Big, googly eyes and a giant smile. Only three teeth, though. Huge feet with four toes. And she was holding a daisy."

He easily imagined young Melinda patting the family troll for luck. "Where's Helga now?"

"After Grandma died, Mom took her." Her shoulders rose and fell in a shrug. "Maybe Helga will come home with me. To bring good luck to the baby."

Drew had no experience with family traditions, but he liked the idea of a troll being passed down through the generations. "Is there some kind of ritual to call for Helga's good luck?"

"Not really. She just watches over us like a guardian angel." She turned toward him. "Why are you asking? Is there a special need for luck?"

"There are a limited number of bridges crossing the Missouri. If people are watching for us, they'll be at one of these points."

"But probably at Interstate 90."

"That's what I'm hoping."

The odds were with them, but he was cautious as he merged into the lanes of cars and trucks approaching the heavy girders of the bridge.

"The mighty Missouri," she said as she peered through the window. "I always think of crossing a bridge as a symbolic change. My life is taking a different course."

As was his. Her pregnancy affected them both. He was going to be a father. No turning back.

On the opposite side of the bridge, he breathed more easily. Everything seemed to be going according to his carefully laid plans. After they made a stop at the garage he'd rented outside Pierre, they'd be untrackable.

At the outskirts of the town, Melinda spoke up. "Did you see the motorcycle? The rider had a black helmet with lightning bolts. Just like the guy in Rapid City."

Drew couldn't believe they'd been followed. He'd taken back roads, doubled back and circled around. Had the motorcyclist been waiting for them here? How had he known their route? "It can't be the same guy."

"He's right behind us."

At the corner, Drew turned left and slowed, hoping the motorcycle would stay on the main road.

No such luck. The Harley roared as he came close to Drew's bumper.

They were within a couple of miles of the garage. Too close to fail. Drew hit the gas. Using every trick he learned from Grand Prix racing, he darted from one street to the next until they were in open countryside.

He raced toward a crossroads with a gas station on one corner. The motorcycle still followed.

"Slow down," Melinda yelled.

From the gas station, a black sedan shot toward the intersection. If Drew continued to go forward, he'd be trapped between the motorcycle and the sedan with no room to escape.

He cranked the steering wheel and hit the brakes. They went into a controlled spin.

The sedan swung toward them.

They were hit.

The impact crushed the driver's side of the SUV.

Chapter Seven

Melinda's air bag exploded, throwing her backward against the seat. She was pinned for a few seconds, not long enough for her whole life to flash before her eyes. But she saw her grandma. And Helga the troll. And a child, a little boy who looked like Drew. *Their child.*

Coughing and flailing desperately, she fought her way free from the air bag. Her ears still rang with the horrible, grinding crash of metal against metal.

"Drew," she shouted. "Drew, are you—"

His air bag hadn't deployed. He was slumped over the steering wheel. The collar of his white shirt was drenched with blood from a head wound. His blue sweater was stained. So much blood! He wasn't moving.

Was he dead? Her heart plummeted. *No, this can't be.* "Drew, wake up."

Through his shattered window, she saw the car

that hit them. The hood had popped open. The engine spewed white smoke.

She batted the air bag out of the way. Through the windshield, she saw the motorcycle wheel around and park in front of them. The rider in the lightning-bolt helmet dismounted. He strode toward them.

Drew jolted upright in his seat. He growled, "Are you all right?"

"Thank God, you're alive."

"And I mean to stay that way."

He twisted the key in the ignition, and she heard their engine start up. The main impact of the crash had been on the driver's-side door. Their car was drivable.

Though it was obvious that Drew was in pain, he grasped the steering wheel with his right hand. They lurched forward, headed directly toward the man who had been on the motorcycle.

Drew's intention was clear. He meant to run this man down. To kill him before he killed them.

Though she didn't want to watch, she couldn't look away. At the last instant, the motorcycle man, still wearing his helmet, leaped out of the way.

Drew kept going. He sideswiped the motorcycle, taking it out of commission.

Digging under the air bag, she found her purse. She took out her cell phone and turned it on.

"What are you doing?" Drew asked.

"Calling the police."

"Don't."

Blood streaked down his forehead. It was a miracle that he was even conscious. "You need to go to a hospital. We need help."

"Let me do this my way."

Her fingers clenched on the cell phone, itching to punch in three easy numbers. Nine-one-one. But he didn't want to involve the police, and she was learning to trust his judgment. She turned it back off and let the phone slip back into her purse.

"At least let me drive," she said. "You're injured."

"Later. We're almost there."

To the cabin? She thought it was tucked away in the Black Hills. "Where?"

"Give me five minutes."

He seemed to know where he was going. As he drove, the SUV shuddered. Wind rushed through the shattered window on the driver's side. He turned onto a dirt road leading toward a deserted farmhouse. It didn't look like anyone had lived here in a very long time. The paint was chipped and peeling. A screen door hung open on the hinges. A rusted swing set stood under a huge, leafless cottonwood tree by the back door. Behind the house, Drew pulled up to the double doors of a small barn that was just as ramshackle as the deserted house.

He took a set of keys from his pocket. "One of these opens the lock on the side door. When you're inside, these other keys open the locks on the double doors."

She grabbed the keys, jumped from the car and ran toward the barn. Though the sedan and motorcycle had appeared to be too damaged to follow them, she imagined the pursuit coming closer. The hairs on the back of her neck prickled.

She fitted the key into the door lock and pushed it open. Inside, it was dark, and she fumbled around until she found a light switch. A couple of bare lightbulbs illuminated the interior.

A vehicle was parked inside. A classic, two-door Range Rover with heavy-duty tires for going off-road. A guy she'd dated in high school had a similar, no-frills manly car that he liked a whole lot more than he had liked her.

Drew must have been keeping the Rover here for his escape, knowing that his SUV could be tracked and followed. Talk about foresight! He really had planned for every contingency.

She went to the double doors. From the outside, the barn looked beat-up and vacant. In here, there were two hinged locks and a thick chain holding the doors shut. When she had everything unfastened, she pushed the heavy barn door open so he could drive inside.

Through his shattered window, he called to her. "Close the doors behind me."

Though she did as he instructed, Melinda was about to take charge. She knew that he'd managed to drive here on sheer guts and determination. Now it was her turn to step up. She needed to get him to a doctor, whether he liked it or not.

She pulled the door shut as soon as the SUV was inside. Though he turned the engine off, a gaseous smell permeated the musty scent inside the barn. They were lucky—*thank you, Helga*—to have made it this far. She stalked across the concrete slab floor to the SUV.

Since the driver's-side door was too damaged to open, Drew maneuvered himself onto the passenger seat. He sat for a moment, still and quiet.

She opened the door and leaned inside. "Are you okay? Can I get you anything?"

"Water."

Earlier, they'd stopped at a gas station, and she'd picked up a six-pack of bottled water. She opened the back door, took one of the bottles and unfastened the screw top before she placed it in his hand.

He tilted his head back as he drank, draining half the bottle in a few gulps. "I'm going to have one hell of a headache."

"At the very least," she said. "I'm worried about your injuries. You need to see a doctor."

"Not really."

When he peeled off his sweater, she saw the left side of his body for the first time. His sleeve was torn and bloody. After that crash, she wouldn't have been surprised if his arm was broken, but he seemed to have full range of movement. He unbuttoned his shirt and took it off. The white T-shirt underneath was only lightly spattered with blood. Using the remaining water from the bottle, he dampened the cotton shirt he'd been wearing. Using the rearview mirror, he wiped the blood from his face. "Have we got more water?"

She handed him another bottle, and he carelessly sloshed water over his head.

"Stop it." She took the shirt from his hand. "Let me clean the wound. You're going to make it worse."

"Are you a nurse?"

"I know basic first aid and CPR." It occurred to her that he might be in shock. "Maybe you should get in the back of the SUV and lie down."

"We need to keep moving." He swung his legs around and climbed out of the SUV. "The longer we're in this area, the more likely we'll be discovered."

Though he appeared to be steady on his feet,

she figured that he could be operating on an adrenaline rush. Later, he'd collapse, and his injuries would take their toll.

Firmly, she clasped his right arm. "You're coming with me, mister. Before we do anything else, I need to take care of you."

She led him to a plain wooden bench against the front of the barn. Everything was covered in dust. Not the world's most sanitary conditions, but it couldn't be helped. She sat him down on the bench. Using his shirt, she dabbed gently at his forehead. Though the skin at his left temple was heavily bruised and swollen, she couldn't find the abrasion.

"There has to be a cut," she said. The blood that saturated his shirt and sweater came from somewhere. Carefully, she examined his scalp. No wound. "I don't understand."

When she looked into his face, his green eyes were serious. "I didn't want you to find out like this."

"Find out what?" She lightly probed the bruise on his forehead. "Does that hurt?"

"A little," he admitted.

She poured more water on the shirt and wiped the black-and-blue area on his skull. The swelling seemed to be going down, but that was impossible. He'd been injured less than an hour ago.

As she watched, the dark edges of discoloration faded to a normal skin color. "What's going on?"

"Remember when I told you about the blackouts I had as a kid?"

"Of course I remember." She couldn't take her gaze off his forehead. The bruise was visibly receding.

"I believe," he said, "that I was part of an experiment. They did something to my blood, causing it to have regenerative properties."

"What are you saying?"

"My body heals itself. Within minutes, any injury is gone."

Unbelievable! But the evidence was right here. Before her eyes, his bruise had disappeared.

Stunned, she sank down on the bench beside him. Had the world turned upside down? *Am I as crazy as Drew?* Her throat constricted. She couldn't breathe.

His arm encircled her and pulled her close. "The men who are after me want to finish their experiments."

Resting her head on his chest, she listened to the strong, steady thump of his heart. He was solid and warm, undeniably real. And able to heal himself? His body had regenerative properties?

She had no idea how to deal with this information, how to deal with him. He was some kind of miracle. "Either I've slipped into an alternate universe or you're telling the truth."

"Believe it," he said.

She pulled herself together. Later, she'd sort fact from fiction. Right now, they needed to make tracks.

FOR THE FIRST TIME in his life, Drew had revealed the secret that ruled his life. In spite of the throbbing headache that always accompanied his self-healing, he felt relieved as he drove westward into the rolling landscape that led to the Black Hills. "As soon as I'm sure we're safe," he said, "I want you to drive."

"Sure," she said. "You look tired."

"That's the downside to being able to heal myself. Afterward, I'm tired and have a killer headache."

"Why?"

"I haven't actually consulted a doctor, but—"

"Why not?" she interrupted.

"I've spent my whole adult life running from people who want to experiment on me. If I handed myself over to an M.D., I'd be volunteering to be a subject. Written up in medical journals as Patient X. Giving endless blood samples. Constantly poked and probed."

"Not necessarily. You could find someone sympathetic."

"I won't be treated like a freak."

His deepest fear. He'd never before spoken the words aloud, but the dread was always with him. He wasn't like other people. Not normal. And if he wasn't careful, he'd end up in a cage.

He felt the gentle touch of her hand on his arm. Her voice dropped to a feather-soft tone. "I can't really say that I understand. It's all too new to me. But I respect your decision. No doctors. No policemen."

He appreciated her honesty. The drumming ache inside his skull took on a hard, driving, heavy-metal rhythm. He needed to rest. "It might help me stay awake if you talked. Do you have questions?"

"Only about ten thousand or so," she said. "Let's start with the process. How does it work?"

"I heal through my blood. When I'm injured, my regenerative blood rushes to the site. Which means that the rest of my body, including my brain, is momentarily starved. As a result, I end up with a killer headache and a need to sleep."

"Can you feel pain?"

"Hell, yes."

"So you're not like those lizards that can grow another tail," she said. "Of course you're not. You don't have scales. And you're warm-blooded."

"One hundred percent mammal."

She kept the questions coming. "When did you first know that you could heal yourself?"

"It happened after the first couple of times I had blackouts. I was ten. Belle had left me alone in the kitchen, and there were cookies in the oven." He still remembered that enticing smell. "I used a pot holder, but the cookie sheet slipped and I burned my hand."

He'd known that Belle would be angry, so he ran to his room to hide. "It was a pretty deep burn. At first, it hurt like hell. Then the pain changed to a stinging sensation. I held up my hand and watched it heal before my eyes."

"That must have freaked you out. Did you tell your foster parents?"

"Hell, no." Belle had him terrified that he'd be taken away and locked up in a dark asylum. "I didn't understand what was happening to me. I didn't really understand what it meant to self-heal until I was older and got into sports."

"Aha!" She sat up straighter in her seat. "Now I know why you're not afraid to try extreme sports. You can't be injured."

He wanted to keep talking to her, but the ripples of exhaustion were becoming a tidal wave. And the drumming inside his head was deafening. He pulled onto the shoulder of the road. "You're driving."

He barely had the strength to drag himself out of the car and change places with her. After giving her brief instruction, he leaned back against the seat. He wanted to believe that his precautions had outsmarted the men who were following him. They wouldn't be looking for this vehicle. They didn't know the location of his cabin.

Though he tried to stay awake to make sure she was able to negotiate the back roads to the interstate, he faded quickly into a semiconscious state. Memories he'd forgotten flowed through his mind. Times and places he barely recalled flashed in vivid color. As quickly as they appeared, the images were erased until only one remained. An eight-pointed star.

He'd seen it before.

Chapter Eight

The hum of the truck's engine and the gentle motion of highway driving soothed the anxieties that had been Drew's constant companion throughout his adult life. His secrets, now revealed, seemed even more dangerous because Melinda was involved.

He yawned. "How long was I asleep?"

She checked her Swiss Army wristwatch. "One hour and fifty minutes."

She'd found Interstate 90. They were headed west toward the Black Hills, making good time. His escape plan had always been to travel this leg on the highway after he ditched his car and switched to the Range Rover—a vehicle purchased under an alias that had no connection to him.

Though he should have been awake and alert, Melinda appeared to be doing a fine job. She sat upright with perfect posture. Her hands on the steering wheel were at ten and two, just the way a driver's-education instructor would recommend. Her eyes were glued to the road, and he had no doubt that she was a good driver, law-abiding and careful.

He'd been worried about how she'd react to his ability. She could have been repulsed or shocked or scared. Instead, she'd come through like a champ. Right away, she figured out that the most important factor was that they escape.

She was his partner, and it felt damn good to have somebody on his team.

She cast a glance in his direction. "How are you feeling?"

"Good." The sleep refreshed him. His headache had faded to a mere twinge. Physically, he was back to one hundred percent. "I've found that head injuries tend to heal quickly with few aftereffects."

"Have you had concussions before?"

"Frequently."

She pointed through the windshield to a roadside sign advertising Wall Drugs. "Get Wall-eyed at Wall," she read. "We're stopping there."

"At the drug store. Why?"

"I've been reading those signs for the past hour and I'm dying for a hot dog." She cocked her head to one side, curious and adorable. "What happens if you don't eat? Would your body keep you from starving to death?"

"Never tried it."

"What about the opposite? Do your abilities keep you from getting flabby? If that's true, I'd like a transfusion, please."

Joking about his ability was new to him. He'd always taken himself seriously. "I don't experiment on myself."

"Aren't you curious? Don't you want to jump off a bridge or shoot yourself to see if you can heal?"

"I feel the pain," he reminded her.

"Oh, yeah. Right."

He watched her profile as she drove. Her milky complexion glowed against her light auburn hair. Though strands had fallen from her high ponytail to curl around her ears, she still looked neat. She'd pushed up the sleeves of her sweater, hiding the stains left by his blood.

He was fairly certain that his own appearance wasn't so normal. The blood spatters stood out on his white T-shirt. "Pull over at the next rest stop so we can wash up and get changed."

"I'd rather stop at a gas station so I can get something to eat."

He pondered for a moment. Any kind of stop was dangerous because it meant exposure. Somehow, his pursuers had known he'd cross the Missouri at Pierre. They might have eyes at gas stations. But they needed fuel. "Okay, next gas station. We can't stop to have a real meal, but it wouldn't hurt to grab a couple of sandwiches."

"No Wall Drugs?" she asked.

"Too many witnesses."

"Okeydokey." She shrugged. "I'm new at being on the run. New at all of this, and I still have a lot of unanswered questions."

"Shoot."

"I want more examples," she said.

He decided against mentioning the recent incident on the cliffs outside Naples. There was no need to remind her of the danger. "There was a scuba diving incident when I got cut pretty bad on a coral reef. And a spectacular crash on a motorcycle. One time, when I was skiing on a glacier, I took a bad fall and banged up my noggin pretty good."

"Of course, you weren't wearing a helmet."

"Why should I?"

"Good point," she conceded. "I'm beginning to see a pattern here. You're that guy who always walks away from disaster without a scratch."

"Some people say I'm the luckiest man on earth."

"But what do you say?"

He wasn't so sure. His ability to self-heal had saved his sorry butt many times, and he was grateful to have survived. But his regenerative blood made him the object of a manhunt that had been going on since he left the Andersons' house on his eighteenth birthday. He was a freak. Isolated.

He wasn't sure if his ability was a blessing or a curse, but he couldn't imagine being any other way. Since he was ten, he'd been different. And his ability led him into a lifestyle he thoroughly enjoyed. "If I hadn't been able to heal myself, I wouldn't have survived those early years in New York when I was working two jobs and going to school. I never got more than a couple of hours of sleep a night."

"Hold it," she said. "Can you heal exhaustion?"

"Pretty much. Depleting your body's natural reserves is like an injury."

"I like it," she said emphatically. "You can stay up all night."

"But I love sleeping." Allowing his systems to shut down and his brain to fade into slumber was an incredible luxury. "It's almost as good as sex."

"That's a topic I want to discuss," she said. "Intercourse."

Her prim manner amused him. "What about it?"

"As you know, I'm on the pill and we only made love once when you didn't use a condom. I'm thinking that you have exceptionally hardy sperm. Your little guys are like superheroes in capes and masks. Indestructible. That's how I got pregnant."

"Interesting theory."

"Yeah, well, I'm not sure I like the idea of being invaded by an army of supersperm. The next time we make love, I might just pull out the kryptonite."

She'd said "next time," which he translated to "maybe tonight." He couldn't wait.

WHEN THEY GOT TO the Black Hills, night had fallen. The mountainous terrain closed around them in an embrace as they went deeper and deeper into the pine forests. Melinda had lost track of all the twists and turns on their way to the remote cabin.

Apparently, when Drew went into hiding, he didn't kid around. For the past ten minutes on a winding two-lane road, she hadn't seen a single light or mailbox or any other sign of human habitation.

Though she'd come to grips with the idea that Drew wasn't crazy, their current situation ranked as one of the most bizarre she'd ever encountered, and that was saying something because she'd read tons of fiction. At least there weren't green aliens with six arms involved...she hoped.

Applying common sense to Drew's theory that he'd been experimented on as a teenager, she was still trying to draw logical conclusions.

"There had to be a reason why you were chosen," she said. "Something biological or genetic."

"Since I'm an orphan, there isn't a good way to check my family background."

"Did you look for your parents?"

"I tracked my way to a dead end. Literally." He peered through the windshield at the edge of the thick forest. "As far as I can tell, I have no living relatives."

"What about your biological parents?"

"Not much to tell. This was almost thirty years ago, before every person had an Internet profile. My father was a pilot in the air force, stationed right here in South Dakota at Ellsworth AFB. He met my mother, a high school math teacher, in Rapid City. Three years after I came along, they were killed in a plane crash. It was a small plane with no black box, and the FAA called it an accident due to weather conditions."

"So you were three when they died," she said. "Do you have any memory of them?"

"I remember my mother singing. She'd get down on her knees, hold my hands and dance with me. I wish there was more. A scrapbook or a toy. Something."

The wistful tone in his voice touched Melinda's heart. Even though he was too young to remember much, the tragedy of losing both parents must have been terrible.

"When I was a kid," he said, "I used to imagine that they'd come back. I hoped the report of their death was a mistake, and there was some other reason they couldn't be with me. I guess that's a common fantasy for orphans."

She wanted to wrap her arms around him and comfort him. Children needed to have parents or, at least, someone who loved them unconditionally. She would make certain that the child growing inside her would know both her and Drew. Even if they weren't together.

"Have you seen health records for your parents?"

"I accessed the military reports on my father, who was in excellent physical condition. Perfect vision. Blond hair. Blue eyes. I couldn't get into my mother's records."

"Basically, you're telling me that there's no way of knowing if your biological parents had any sort of genetic anomaly."

"Correct." He slowed and turned onto a graded gravel road that was almost invisible. "One more mile to go."

Settling down in his cabin sounded terrific to her. Though she'd grabbed a couple of sandwiches at the gas station, she was still hungry for something sweet. He'd told her that there were food supplies at the cabin. But would there be chocolate?

"I assume you've done research on the people who experimented on you," she said. "They must have had a screening process to pick you."

"I always figured that being in foster care made me an easy target. There wasn't anybody to protect me."

"What about the Andersons?"

"I'm pretty sure they were paid off to keep their mouths shut while I was being tested."

He drove slowly on the one-lane road. In some parts, it was so narrow that the pine branches brushed the side of the Range Rover. There were no neighbors anywhere in sight. "How did you find this place?"

"On the Internet."

"Under real estate listings for hermits?"

The road widened into a clearing. Moonlight spilled across the dull winter grass in front of a small log house surrounded by forest. The windows were closed with wood shutters, making the one-story cabin, with its sloped, shake shingle roof, look like it was sleeping with eyes closed. A stone fireplace rose from one end.

Behind the cabin and nearly as big was a garage that looked as if it had been newly constructed and painted a dark brown. She wondered what kind of vehicle he'd stashed in there.

Drew pulled up to the front door. "We'll unload first, then I'll put the Range Rover away."

She hauled in her own suitcase and a bag of groceries from the gas station convenience store, where they'd stopped hours ago.

The interior was one large room with a stone fireplace against one wall and a kitchenette on the opposite side. The warmth of knotty pine paneling contrasted with the on-the-run technology and weaponry she was coming to associate with Drew. Three white-topped tables were covered with computers, monitors, printers, cameras and other unfathomable electronics.

As soon as they entered, Drew flipped a couple of switches by the door. "It'll be warm in a few minutes. I replaced the propane heater with an electric generator and radiant heat."

"What about the fireplace?"

"Never use it. Smoke rising from the chimney would give away the location."

Instead of thinking he was the victim of paranoid delusion, she appreciated his attention to detail. They needed every advantage. She glanced around the room. The furniture was minimal. Only one office chair and a mattress on the floor. Hopefully, she asked, "Is there an attached bedroom?"

"Afraid not. I never expected to have company."

"What about a bathroom? Please tell me there's a bathroom."

He opened a door. "It's got a flush toilet and everything. The cabin has its own well, so water isn't a problem. But I use a small water heater to conserve energy."

"Not a lot of hot water," she suggested.

"There's enough." He grinned. "If we shower together."

When it came to making love, she wasn't quite sure how she felt. Of course, she was attracted to him. Any warm-blooded, breathing woman would be. But they'd been so busy running that there hadn't been time to talk about their future.

She dropped her suitcase near the mattress and went to the kitchenette. The refrigerator had a six-pack of beer, ketchup and a jar of pickles. "Good golly, there has to be more food."

He unfastened a latch on a door that blended into the knotty pine paneling. "The pantry."

She stepped inside. Floor-to-ceiling shelves held canned goods and a depressing variety of packaged food, ranging from instant potatoes to coffee. None of it appealed to her until she spied a stack of extra-large chocolate bars and grabbed one off the top. "Mine."

"We could have stew," he said, lifting a can

with an overly bright picture of beef and carrots on the front.

"Maybe later."

Melinda wasn't picky about her food. She didn't require gourmet cuisine and was accustomed to making do with a little bit of this and that. Nor did she have qualms about living arrangements. Until she got the apartment in Sioux Falls, she'd always lived with someone else— her sisters or roommates or dorm mates in college. That meant dealing with messes that weren't hers.

But this cabin was one step up from a bomb shelter with very little charm and zero amenities. The mattress on the floor had only a sleeping bag. No sheets. No comforter.

In the back of her mind, she'd been hoping for a little romance—a chance to talk to Drew about the pregnancy in pleasant surroundings where they could relax. She plunked down on the double-size mattress and nibbled at the edge of her candy bar. The cabin would have been so much nicer with a roaring fire.

Drew joined her. "You're disappointed."

"It's okay." She heard the break in her voice. As if she was going to burst into tears? What kind of spoiled brat was she? She hoisted a determined smile onto her face. "Really, I understand. This is a hideout. Not a five-star hotel. We need to focus on the bad guys."

"I have another sleeping bag in the storage room," he said. "There's only one pillow, but—"

"We'll be fine," she said with as much enthusiasm as she could muster. "There's food, water and a roof over our heads. Roughing it will be fun."

"You don't have to convince me."

She was convincing herself, trying to make the best of things. "Let's get back to what we were talking about in the car."

"And what was that?"

She'd been following a train of thought that was relatively logical. Drew had been given a remarkable ability. "Even though you don't remember anything about the experiments, they must have taken place in a hospital or a lab."

"Which I've never located. A secret facility."

"Considering that this was taking place decades ago, before the idea of cloning and mapping the genome was commonplace, these experiments were using cutting-edge science."

"Very much so." He reached toward her. With his thumb, he wiped at the corner of her mouth. "You had a smudge of chocolate."

When he drew his hand back and licked his thumb, she focused on his lips. She knew what it was like to have his mouth on her body, knew the pleasure that resulted when he trailed kisses down her throat to her breasts to her belly.

Forcing herself to look away, she came to her logical conclusion. "A scientist wouldn't use just one subject. There had to be a test group. That means you're not the only person who can self-heal."

"Not necessarily," he said. "With me, the experiment was successful. They could have tried with others. And failed."

She shuddered at the thought of other children who were stolen from their homes and never awoke from the blackouts. "But if they had such a terrible success rate, the experiments wouldn't have continued. How long did they work with you?"

"Eight years."

"There have to be others like you," she said. "And we need to find them."

Chapter Nine

While Melinda washed up in the bathroom, Drew activated the security measures at the cabin. Similar to the setup in his apartment, he had surveillance cameras—four of them—placed strategically around the cabin to observe the approach of intruders. Motion sensors on the road were calibrated to indicate the approach of a vehicle.

Since it was after dark, he didn't bother opening the shutters that covered the windows. There would be no lights shining from the cabin.

In the storage room next to the bathroom, he found his second sleeping bag. He unzipped both and spread them on the double mattress. Melinda deserved satin sheets and downy comforters, but this would have to do.

Her reasoning that there were others like him wasn't a new idea for him. Years ago, he'd been convinced that he wasn't the only person who had undergone treatments that gave him special abilities. Though he didn't know where he was taken during his blackouts, it couldn't have been far from his hometown of Lead. Other subjects had to live nearby. He'd thought they might even attend his high school.

And so, he studied the other guys, especially those who were athletic. If they got bruised or sick, he eliminated them, until he narrowed the list to one. His name was Mark Terrance. Mark's parents were separated, and he spent most weekends in Rapid City with his father. Or did he? Those frequent absences could have been times when he was taken to the secret facility.

Drew wanted to find out about Mark, but the urgency of his quest took a backseat to his love for Erica Clark. His first girlfriend reminded him of Melinda. They both had curly hair and great smiles. Both were smart and funny. Both liked sex. Not that he'd gone beyond second base with Erica.

He'd wanted to tell her about his ability, his affliction. But he was too afraid of losing her. His plan was to wait until after they'd made love. That day never came.

When Erica was killed in a car accident, Drew felt like his still-beating heart had been torn from his body. He couldn't eat or sleep or think or even cry.

The whole high school showed up for her funeral. People who barely knew her sobbed in the church pews. People she'd hated wrung their hands in fake mourning. Drew kept his sorrow inside, unseen and festering; he vowed to never fall in love again.

After her burial, Mark came up to Drew in the cemetery, punched him on the arm and told him to lighten up. Maybe his intentions were good, but Drew didn't want to talk to anybody. When he tried to walk away, Mark stayed at his side, babbling about some upcoming sports event.

Drew grabbed him by the collar and said, "I know about you. About your secret."

Mark got red in the face. "I don't have any secrets."

"You're like me."

"Damn, I hope not."

To prove his point, Drew cocked his arm and snapped a quick jab to Mark's jaw. He went down, grazing his cheek on the edge of a gravestone. Blood slashed across his face.

They were quickly separated by the other mourners. The next day, Mark had stitches on his face. The wound had not healed; Mark wasn't like him.

In that moment, Drew knew he was alone.

But not anymore. Melinda was here with him.

He looked toward the closed bathroom door. From inside, he heard the shower running.

She peeked through the door and grinned. "Well, Drew? Aren't you going to join me?"

He leaped from the mattress. Half his clothes were off by the time he got to the bathroom door.

MELINDA DODGED back into the bathroom and slipped behind the shower curtain. The beige-tiled stall was small but well-scrubbed, which she truly appreciated. Drew's cabin had minimal accommodations, but it was clean. She tilted her head back so the hot water flowed through her hair, rinsing away the dirt from the road.

Inviting Drew to join her might have been a huge mistake. She couldn't allow herself to start thinking that they'd be together on a long-term basis. They'd made no commitments, hadn't exchanged any kind of promises. Neither of them had spoken of love. She cautioned herself to remember: *We're lovers. But not in love.*

She couldn't be with a man who thrived on danger, especially not when she was pregnant. And she would never drag a child into that kind of life.

Not that she blamed Drew for their current problems. He was as much of a victim as she was in this situation. Still, they were on the run from mysterious villains who attacked her in her apartment, erased her memory, chased them from

Sioux Falls and crashed into them on the road. *Was all this really happening?* It felt like she'd stumbled through a secret door into a world of espionage. Pretty darn exciting, she had to admit. But definitely not the way she wanted to live.

He stepped into the shower with her. In the small tiled cubicle, there was no escaping him. And she didn't want to try. If there was a possibility that they'd be killed tomorrow, she might as well enjoy tonight.

Her breasts grazed his muscular chest, and he pulled her more tightly against him. The steam from the hot water wrapped around them in a moist cloud.

His kiss was demanding and fierce, awakening a surge of passion in her. Her inhibitions washed away. Making love to Drew transformed her. In everyday life, she was a down-to-earth woman. With him, she was a regular sex goddess. Her tongue plunged into his mouth, tasting him, craving him.

Their wet, slick bodies slithered against each other. His erection pressed against her belly as he maneuvered her around so the shower water beat against his back.

His voice was husky. "I didn't think you'd invite me in."

"Neither did I."

"What changed your mind?"

She slid her hand down his lean flank. The man was all muscle. "I was being practical," she said.

"How so?"

"I figured since we have to sleep in the same bed, we'd probably end up making love. Might as well start here so we don't waste the warm water."

A chuckle rumbled in his throat. "You're one hot librarian, Melinda."

She reached for the soap. "We should wash ourselves before the water runs out."

"Very practical."

She soaped up his chest, creating sudsy swirls in his light sprinkling of chest hair. Then, she washed his rock-hard abdomen. When she touched his sex, he tensed. She reveled in her power to excite him, and she teased with light strokes and pinches.

He took the soap from her. When he washed her breasts, she trembled. Her nipples were hard and exquisitely sensitive. She gasped.

"Am I hurting you?"

"Yes," she said. "But don't stop."

Her breasts felt heavy and swollen. *Because I'm pregnant.* Sensual electricity raced through her. This was an unexpected but delightful by-product of her condition.

When he turned her around to face the shower, she asked, "What are you doing?"

He picked up a bottle of shampoo. "Washing your hair."

The foamy lather dripped over her shoulders as he massaged her scalp. If this sensation could be duplicated in a beauty parlor, she'd be a weekly patron.

Though he carefully rinsed her hair, she asked, "What about conditioner?"

"This is one of those shampoos that have both."

A man's shampoo. Her hair needed more, but tomorrow's frizz was a small price to pay for the ripples of arousal that came when he glided his arms around her and cupped her breasts. His erection slid between her buttocks.

The hot water had begun to run out. She turned off the faucet. "Let's take this to the bed."

After drying quickly, she rushed to the mattress and snuggled between the two sleeping bags. Drew turned off all the lights except for one over the computer. The screens showed black-and-white pictures of the forest. Surveillance cameras like the ones in his apartment. The danger that drove them to this cabin was still a threat.

He joined her under the sleeping bag. His hair was still wet, as was hers. It occurred to her that she should run a comb through it. Had he packed her blow dryer?

"What's wrong?" he asked.

"I'm going to get everything soppy with my hair."

He returned to the bathroom and came back with a fresh towel, which he spread under her head. "Problem solved."

She glanced toward the computer screens. "Do you think they'll find us?"

"I've taken every possible precaution. We should be safe." Still, he looked worried. "But I don't underestimate them. I never thought they'd pick up our trail in Pierre."

"A lucky guess?"

"I don't believe in luck." He stroked her damp hair off her face. "Except for Helga the troll."

"She's watching over us."

He pushed aside the sleeping bag, baring her upper body. His fingers traced a line between her breasts. On her belly he drew a light circle.

She closed her eyes. His gentle touch reignited the flame of passion, and she sighed with pleasure. "You're writing something on my belly."

"Am I?"

"You've done that before," she said dreamily. "Always the same pattern. What is it?"

"An eight-pointed star. It's an image that keeps popping into my head. I don't know the meaning."

"I think it means you're supposed to kiss me. Eight times."

He started on her forehead. Then, her left ear. Then, her throat. These were slow, nibbling kisses—erotic tickles. He lingered on each breast, teasing her nipples. He kissed lower, and she arched her back.

Kiss number eight landed on her mouth, and she opened herself to him. He rose above her, parting her thighs. The tip of his erection probed between her legs. She needed to take him inside her.

"Condom?" he asked.

"Damage already done," she said, vaguely recalling their earlier conversation. She didn't care if he sent thousands of supersperm into her body. In fact, she welcomed them. "I want you now."

He entered her with a thrust, and she rose up to meet him, pulling him deeper inside her. *More, I want more.* To be joined to him, a part of him. Her need became aggressive, demanding. She arched against him. Her fingernails clawed at his back. *No need to worry about scratching him.* He'd heal.

Harder and harder, he drove. She met and matched his passion with her own fierce need, until she exploded. Jagged lightning flashed behind her eyes. An earthquake erupted inside her, sending tremors of pure pleasure through her body.

He collapsed beside her on the sleeping bag. They were both gasping, happily exhausted. She curled up beside him with her head resting on his shoulder.

Blissful sleep and happy dreams should be the aftermath of such perfect lovemaking. She tried to push all the questions from her mind, but her gaze lit on the surveillance cameras. Their lovemaking had not erased the danger.

"Does it ever go away?" she asked. "The threat?"

"Never."

"Then, we might as well deal with it." She exhaled a long sigh. "The eight-pointed star. Have you tried to figure out what it means?"

"A long time ago," he said, "I looked it up online, did a little research. It's a symbol in a lot of different religions and sects, including a possible reference to the Star of Bethlehem. Nothing seemed pertinent."

Mind-blowing sex generally left her as dumb as a stump, reveling in blissful sensation. But her brain was beginning to function. "Sensory memory," she said. "Some people remember things by smell or sound or taste. There's a cue from your senses that translates to an actual memory."

"Like hearing a song that reminds you of the first time you heard it."

She walked her fingers across his chest. "Maybe you have muscle memory. Doing a particular gesture—like drawing that star—reminds you of something. It makes sense that you'd remember with your whole body because you're so…physical."

"That's a damn good theory. You're a pretty smart lady."

"Yes, well, I do a lot of reading." She propped herself up on one elbow and looked into the emerald-green of his eyes. "Let's see what happens if I draw the symbol on you."

He folded his hands behind his head. "Go for it."

Using her fingernail, she outlined a star on his naked belly. The way she would have drawn an eight-point star would have been with two interlocking diamond shapes, but she used the same process he did, making each point separately.

"Does that make you think of anything?"

"I want you again."

"Already?" A thought occurred to her. "This self-healing thing. Does it apply to sex?"

He grinned. "I've always been quick to recover."

Though she wasn't capable of self-healing or any other unusual ability, she was ready to make love again. Tonight was for them alone. She didn't want to think of what tomorrow might bring.

Chapter Ten

Wide awake at half past six o'clock in the morning, Drew kicked off the sleeping bag. The tightly sealed cabin was warm enough that he didn't need covers. Last night, their passion had generated enough heat to melt a glacier. That marathon of lovemaking was something he wouldn't soon forget…unlike all the other blank spaces in his memory.

Melinda was on her side with her back to him. Her creamy skin glowed enticingly. For a moment, he considered trailing a line of kisses along the sweet curve of her spine until she wakened, and they could make love again.

When he touched her back, she shifted position and gave a contented-sounding moan before settling back to sleep. Lightly, he outlined the eight-pointed star between her shoulder blades.

Her idea of muscle memory intrigued him. He was familiar with the concept as it related to sports. Once you learned how to ride a bicycle, your body never forgot how to do it. Could his body be holding thoughts that his mind didn't recall? If so, how could he access those memories?

Usually, he worked with words, typing into a computer. Never before had he attempted to draw what was in his head. If Melinda was right, that might be worth a try.

He left the mattress, grabbed his jeans off the floor where he'd dropped them last night and got partially dressed. Not wanting to wake her, he crept through the cabin. Poking around on the tabletops that held his electronic equipment, he found a couple of pens and some plain white paper. He slipped outside.

Sunrise streaked the skies above the treetops with pink and red. The chilly wind through the pine boughs felt good against his bare chest. He sat down on the porch stoop and balanced the stack of white paper on top of a book. He set the point of the pen on the paper and waited for inspiration.

Art wasn't his thing. He created pictures with his words. In his sports articles, he tried to give color and depth to his reporting. On occasion, he took photographs. But drawing?

Start with what you know. He made the star

and lifted the pen from the paper. Another star. Another. This exercise was getting him nowhere.

Shuffling that paper to the bottom of the stack, he aimed his pen again and started doodling. A cube. A rose, like the one in *The Little Prince*. A tree. His sketches looked like a third-grader had done them.

The door behind him opened, and Melinda stepped outside. Dressed in jeans and a pink sweatshirt, she paused from brushing her hair and held her arms wide as if to embrace the sky. "Wow, it's a beautiful morning."

"Last night was beautiful, too."

"You bet it was." She sat beside him and gave him a familiar kiss on the cheek. "What are you doing?"

"Drawing pictures to find memories. So far the only thing I've learned is that I'm no Rembrandt."

"Oh, I don't know." She held up the paper with the tree. "This style could be called primitive."

"As if a caveman did it?"

"Try another focus for your memory. Something you know. How about drawing a picture of the Andersons' house?"

While she continued to brush her hair, he made a rough sketch of a rectangular, ranch-style house with an isosceles triangle for a roof and a big picture window in front. "There."

"I thought you said you were near a forest. Were there trees near the house?"

He added a leafy maple tree in the front yard and shrubs under the windows. The sidewalk made a straight line from the curb, as did the concrete driveway to the attached garage. These details fixed his mental image of the home where he'd lived for eight years. He drew the basketball hoop on the garage.

"Did you play basketball with your foster dad?" she asked.

"A couple of times."

"Draw it."

On a fresh sheet of paper, he sketched sticklike figures of himself and Harlan. Though his scrawls were pathetically sketchy, his memory filled in the rest. Clearly, he saw Harlan's face and heard him speaking. The words echoed in his brain: *You've had enough.* But that wasn't accurate. Drew spoke the words aloud. "He's had enough."

"Who?" she asked.

"I think it was me. Harlan was telling someone that I'd had enough."

"Who was he talking to?"

"Don't know."

She pulled out a clean sheet of paper. "Show me."

Pressing down hard on the pen, he drew a

square and filled it in, blanking out every trace of white. It was dank and cold, like a cave or a prison with heavy iron bars. Then, a long corridor. Where the hell was he?

He tossed the paper aside but kept sketching. He saw a bright circle, a light above his head like in a doctor's examination room. Pieces of pictures—images that made no coherent sense—formed and vanished as he furiously scribbled, trying to catch them.

When he raised the pen from the paper, the memories slipped back into his subconscious mind. During the time he'd been drawing, the sun had risen. He'd been totally absorbed for over an hour.

Melinda set a mug of instant coffee on the stoop beside him. "Looks like you wrote something," she said.

"Sykes." Drew shook his head. The name meant nothing to him, but it was a damn good place to start his research. "Time to hit the computer."

While he'd been drawing like a madman, she had transformed his bunkerlike cabin into a far more pleasant retreat. The shutters over the windows were open. The sleeping bags on the mattress were neatly smoothed. And she'd put together something resembling breakfast from the odds and ends of groceries they'd bought yesterday and his canned foods.

"Biscuits and white gravy," she said. "With some of that canned stew you seem to like. There must be twenty cans of it in the pantry."

"Looks different in here."

"I'll take that as a compliment." She'd cleared a space on one of the computer tables to use for dining. She sat him down in the only chair. "You should eat something. Or maybe not. Your self-healing body doesn't need food."

"I've gone without eating," he said. "But it uses up my energy reserves."

And he needed to stay at full strength, both physically and mentally. It would have been nice to let Melinda pamper him and turn this rough cabin into a home, but he couldn't lose track of the fact that his enemies were still after them.

"I'd love to go hiking," she said. "The view from those granite cliffs above the cabin must be terrific."

"It's not Mount Rushmore. But it's nice. You can see the snow on the high peaks."

"It's not too cold here. But I know that could change in a minute. March can be a snowy month."

He caught hold of her hand and pulled her onto his lap. His light kiss lingered on her mouth. Reluctantly, he leaned back in the chair and gazed into her lovely face. Her lips were full and slightly swollen from last night's thousand and one kisses. Her eyes sparkled. She'd tamed her curly, light auburn hair by pulling it back in a ponytail. "You look good."

"Thank you, sir," she said with mock primness. "I had a chance to put on a dash of mascara. By the way, you did a great job of packing my toiletries."

"I wanted to make sure you had what you needed. In case we had to run away for a long time."

"That's not going to happen." Her tone became practical. "You can't run away from your problems."

"I've done okay. Managed to evade capture for the past ten years."

"Things are different now." She climbed off his lap. "There's a baby to consider."

And there was Melinda. As long as his enemies knew they could get to him through her, she was in danger. No way in hell would he let her come to harm.

He finished off the breakfast, which was surprisingly good and definitely filling. Then he settled in front of the computer to research.

Melinda stood over his shoulder. "I've heard that computers put out a signal that can be traced."

He scoffed. "Do you think I'd forget such an obvious way of tracking me?"

"I guess not," she said. "I mean, you planned far enough ahead to know you needed a second car. And you've got this cabin all set up like a bunker. It's like your fortress of solitude."

"This computer signal bounces all over the world. Nobody can track it."

He started his Internet queries with the eight-pointed star. Thousands of entries were listed, including a rock band and a cult that claimed to be from the Horse Nebula. He narrowed his search with key words, like *South Dakota* and *experimental research*.

What would it be like to find other people with his abilities? Drew had a strong competitive streak, and he knew it would be hard to decide who was in charge.

He typed in the name *Sykes*.

The image that appeared matched exactly with the eight-pointed star he remembered. He followed it to a Web site.

"This looks promising," Melinda said.

Drew hardly dared to hope. He clicked on the contact button and typed in an innocuous comment about wanting information on experimental research near Lead, South Dakota, ten to fifteen years ago.

The response was immediate—My name is Jack Maddox. Welcome.

Drew typed, Do you know me?

You're like me. You were a subject in an experiment you never agreed to. As a result, you developed an extraordinary ability. I've been expecting to hear from you.

Drew typed, Why?

My ability is pre-cog. I see things before they happen.

"I'll be damned," Drew murmured. It hadn't occurred to him that the experiments might produce different effects.

"Pre-cog," Melinda said. "That's so cool."

Drew typed, Is this site safe?

This communication will be virally destroyed within one minute after we disconnect. Turn off your computer so you won't be affected. We need to meet.

But Drew wanted proof that this wasn't a ploy to lure him into the open. He wrote three words on a piece of paper, then typed in his response. Since you're pre-cog, you must know that I need a password or phrase before I trust you.

After a brief pause, three words appeared on the computer screen—The Little Prince.

It was a match to what he'd written. Drew arranged the meeting for seven o'clock in Rapid City at Brewster's Pub.

SINCE RAPID CITY was only an hour and a half away, they didn't have to depart until much later that afternoon. Melinda convinced Drew to step outside the fortress of solitude and take a hike.

Last night's loving had invigorated her. She kept herself in pretty good shape with regular jogging and walking to work whenever the weather permitted, but she'd never felt so strong and vital. Her legs were so springy that she could hardly keep her sneakers on the ground as she bounded up the rocky slope.

Maybe this sense of intense well-being came from being pregnant. Most women complained of morning sickness, and her stomach had occasionally roiled. But she hadn't thrown up.

She paused at the top of a rise above the cabin and leaned against a tree. Drew stood beside her. His gaze never rested. Endlessly, he searched the trees and granite rocks. She wondered if he was worried about meeting tonight with Jack.

"I have a question, Drew. Why didn't you arrange for Jack to come here to the cabin?"

"This is my safe place. I spent a lot of time and money finding this cabin, refurbishing it and setting up security. Nobody gets to know the location."

"But Jack is like you. He was experimented on."

"I'm not so sure."

She understood how difficult it was for him to trust anyone, but Jack had proved his pre-cog ability by naming *The Little Prince*. What a remarkable skill that was! "I can't wait to meet him. And there must be others. I wonder what their abilities are."

"Hold on." He took her arm and turned her to face him. "I'm not taking you into that meeting. It could be a trap."

"But it's not safe to split up." If that dangerous man with the shaved head came after her, she didn't know what she'd do. "You're my protector."

He grinned. "You make it sound like I'm a knight in shining armor."

"It's not that I'm helpless." Melinda would never cast herself as a damsel in distress. "But I know my limits. I've fired weapons before, but I'm not a sharpshooter. And I don't think I can outrun a motorcycle."

"That motorcycle is dead," he said with grim satisfaction. "I clipped it pretty good when we were making our escape."

She remembered that moment. "It looked like you were going to run that guy down."

"I would have."

When he started climbing again, he made hiking up a steep incline look easy. Though she didn't want to think of Drew as a killer, she knew he wouldn't hesitate to fight back with whatever it took. He was a soldier in a private war, fighting for his own survival. And hers. And that of their baby.

An edge of danger cut through the sunlit day. She couldn't pretend that everything was all right. That Web site proved Drew's theories.

At the top of the last rise, she climbed up beside him onto a granite cliff. Though they were less than a mile away from the cabin, his hideout was invisible in this thickly forested landscape. The granite ledge where they stood was as high as the treetops.

In the distance, higher mountains loomed. The pristine white snow drizzled over the peaks like marshmallow cream on chocolate ice cream. Was she hungry again? While they were in Rapid City, she hoped they could pick up groceries to supplement their food supplies.

Drew pointed to a jutting rock formation on the opposite hill. "That's called the Elephant, excellent for rock climbing."

"Have you ever climbed it?"

"A couple of times."

Of course he'd be a rock climber. She considered that to be a dangerous sport, hanging from precipitous ledges from minuscule fissures and handholds. Most climbers used belaying ropes and followed safety procedures, but she figured that Drew would just set out with no fear of falling.

She stepped closer to the edge to get a better look at the rock shaped like an elephant. Her sneaker caught on a loose bit of granite. She slipped. Her feet went out from under her. Before she could catch herself, she was falling, sliding over the edge while she clawed desperately, trying to save herself.

Chapter Eleven

As soon as he saw what was happening, Drew made a dive toward her. He grabbed for her hand. Their fingers barely touched.

With a frantic yelp, Melinda slipped over the edge.

He heard a thud. Then everything went silent.

He should have kept a closer watch on her, should have held her hand while they climbed. Damn it, they should have stayed inside the cabin where she'd be safe.

He heard a groan.

"Melinda?"

"I'm here."

"Don't move. I'm coming for you."

He could have gone the long way around and climbed safely through the forest, but he wanted to reach her as quickly as possible. With a downward glance, he assessed the face of the granite rock wall to figure the most direct descent.

He swung his legs over the edge. Though he wasn't wearing his rock-climbing boots, his toe found a crack in the surface that was strong enough to hold his weight. He braced himself with handholds. He spied another grip and lowered himself. His muscles strained. His bulky leather jacket wasn't the best outfit for rock climbing. He found another hold. Looking down, he saw it was only four more feet to the ground. Pushing away from the rock, he dropped.

In seconds, he was beside her. She was already sitting up. "I'm okay," she said.

"Are you feeling any pain?"

"Gosh, Drew, what do you think?"

"Sarcasm," he said. "That's a good sign."

His unspoken fear was not only for her but for the fetus she carried. Even a relatively minor fall could do irreparable damage. "How did you land?"

"On my feet, then I fell onto my butt." She forced a brave smile. "At first, I couldn't catch my breath. I guess I knocked the wind out of my lungs."

He felt along her legs and pushed up her jeans to examine her ankles. He squeezed the joint. "Does this hurt?"

"Not a bit." She held up her hands. "I think this is the worst of it."

Both palms were badly abraded, oozing blood and streaked with dirt. Not serious injuries unless they got infected. He needed to get her back to the cabin so he could wash her wounds. Soap and water would have to be enough. He didn't own a first-aid kit and had no idea how to treat another person's injury.

He slipped one arm under her knees and wrapped the other around her upper body. "I'll carry you back to the cabin so we can get you cleaned up."

"Don't be silly. I can walk."

He lifted her off the ground. "You don't need to strain yourself."

But she wriggled until he let her legs drop to the ground. Though she leaned against him for a moment, she quickly stood on her own. She seemed steady enough.

"Listen up, Drew. I'm not a fragile little creature. If we're going to get out of this mess in one piece, you need to know that I'm not helpless."

But she could be hurt. And so could their child. He wrapped one arm around her shoulder and rested his other hand on her belly. "Are you sure everything is all right?"

Her sharp intake of breath sounded like the beginning of a sob. Damn it, had he said something wrong?

She rested her injured hand atop his. "You're thinking about our child."

"Yes."

"Well, I don't have a sonogram handy, but…" Her voice faded to stillness, and she looked down at the ground. A tear spilled down her cheek.

Gently, he wiped away the droplet. "I didn't mean to upset you."

She gazed up at him. "I'm glad that you're concerned about the baby. It means a lot to me."

She didn't look glad. Not with her chin wobbling and her eyes leaking. He'd heard that pregnant women were kind of emotional, kind of scary. "If you're glad, so am I."

"The baby was the first thing I thought about when I fell. But I didn't land on my stomach. And I don't feel any cramping or anything like that."

The fetus was tiny, less than two months old. He knew there was a chance of miscarriage. "Is there anything I can do to help?"

"Walk with me. It's all downhill to the cabin."

He fell into step beside her, watching over her like a mother hawk with her hatchling. If she stumbled, he would catch her before she hit the ground.

"We have a problem," he said. "I don't have any bandages or antiseptic at the cabin."

"Right. Because you don't get injured."

"I never expected anybody else to come here."

"Let's put first-aid supplies on the list of things that we need to get in Rapid City. By the way, I'm most definitely coming with you to the meeting with Jack Maddox."

He'd rather have her stay at the cabin, which was a completely secure location. "You'll be safer here."

"Stranded in the forest?" She shook her head. "I don't like the sound of that. If anybody came after me, I wouldn't have any means of escape."

"I could leave the Range Rover here for you."

"How would you get there?" she asked. "Please don't tell me that you can fly."

"Wish I could, but no. I have a Harley in the garage. I'll ride the bike into Rapid City and be back here by ten o'clock."

"Unless something happens."

He didn't need the dark tone in her voice to remind him of all the things that could go wrong. It was entirely possible that Jack Maddox was working for his enemies. His pre-cog skill proved that he had enhanced abilities, but it said nothing about his loyalty. Meeting with him was a risk.

By the time they reached the cabin, she seemed to have regained the spring in her step. He took her directly to the bathroom so he could clean up her wounds.

"Sit." He pointed to the closed toilet seat.

"Actually, I think I'd be better off handling this by myself. Let me wash off my hands. They don't really hurt too much. There's just a sting."

He turned on the water, adjusted the temperature and hovered over her as she carefully rinsed away the blood and dirt. The skin on the back of her hands was pink and clean. When she turned them over…

She'd healed. The scrapes and scratches had completely disappeared. She held them up in front of her eyes. "I guess I wasn't hurt."

He'd seen the abrasions. The scrapes were bad enough that he'd been worried. "You were injured. Not deep gashes, but scrapes. The skin was broken."

She stared at her palms, flexed her fingers. Under her breath, she muttered, "This isn't right."

Her healing process was exactly the same as his. "You mentioned a stinging sensation."

"It's gone. Doesn't hurt anymore."

Standing behind her, he held her shoulders. "Do you have a headache?"

Dumbly, she nodded.

"It'll fade," he assured her. "You might need a short nap."

Her hands rose to cover her mouth as if to hold back a scream. Her eyes squeezed shut. He could feel the tension in her body. And the fear.

"How?" she demanded. "How could this happen?"

His ability had transferred to her. They were part of each other. He wrapped his arms around her and whispered in her ear. "It's the baby. My DNA is part of your body. You have my abilities."

And that changed everything.

MELINDA STUMBLED to the mattress and collapsed onto the sleeping bags. Drew lay beside her, cradling her against his warm chest. Though she didn't want to sleep, her heartbeat slowed, and her body sank into a state of quiet recuperation.

In what seemed like two minutes, she jolted awake. "How long have I been out?"

"A little over half an hour." Drew sat in front of the computer.

On the screen, she saw some kind of car race. "You're watching sports?"

"I didn't know how long you'd be asleep, and I—"

"My whole life just turned upside down, and you're catching up on NASCAR. Typical male."

She rose from the bed and stalked across the room to the window. Raising her hand, she studied the smooth skin on her palm. No sign of a scar. Not even redness.

"How are you feeling?" he asked.

Her sense of physical well-being had returned. "Fine."

The baby had healed her. It didn't seem biologically possible, but she couldn't dispute the evidence. No wonder she didn't have morning sickness. All along, the baby had been taking care of her. If she'd been more alert, she would have noticed the changes before now.

Her first clue should have been when she didn't need her glasses. Her eyesight had improved, thanks to the regenerative quality of Drew's DNA that was now flowing through her blood. And her bruises after she'd been attacked in her apartment had vanished overnight. Another big, fat clue that she'd ignored.

She had to face the fact that she was as indestructible as Drew himself.

And she should have been happy. Who wouldn't be thrilled to know they had special abilities? *Me, that's who*. Having this miraculous power was unsettling.

When Drew told her about his self-healing abilities, she hadn't understood the implications. Being different didn't seem like such a bad thing, especially since the trade-off meant that he could take any risk and heal himself. *But I don't want to be different*.

She'd spent her whole life fitting in with everybody else. Though she didn't particularly value conformity, she appreciated the security. It was good to be accepted. To be a nice person, friendly and practical. People were comfortable around her.

That normal lifestyle was gone forever. Never again would her life be an open book. She had a secret ability that she couldn't share with anyone, except Drew.

"I can't tell anyone."

"Probably not a good idea," he said.

But she'd always told her family everything. They shared triumphs and disasters. "My mom will know. I've never been able to keep secrets from her."

"Never? Have you told her about me? About the baby?"

"Not yet. But I would have."

Clearly, the baby had inherited Drew's genetic makeup. Raising a child that could self-heal was, in many ways, a relief. She wouldn't have the same fears as other mothers.

At the same time, she had to make sure no one found out. Or else her baby would be experimented on. She would never let that happen. No matter what it took, she'd keep this secret.

"If your enemies find out about the baby," she said, "they'll want to take him—"

"Or her," Drew said. "Could be a girl."

"I know that." She whipped around to face him.

"It's a good thing I have this ability because I'll fight to the death to keep them away from my baby."

"Our baby." He rose from the computer and came toward her. "We'll go somewhere far away, somewhere they can't find us."

"But I want our baby to have a fun childhood. To play with other kids. To know my parents and my sisters." She stepped into his embrace. "All of a sudden, going back to Sioux Falls and working at the library seems like the greatest life in the world."

He gently stroked her back. "If that's what you want, we can make that happen."

She realized that he'd said *they* could make it happen. "We" can. As in both of them. Did that mean he'd stay with her? On what basis?

Last night, she'd been subconsciously hoping that he'd drop to one knee and propose. Now, she wasn't so sure.

Her hands drew into fists. She didn't know what she wanted. "Is it selfish to keep this a secret? The regenerative properties in your blood might be able to heal others."

"I've thought about that," he said. "If our privacy could be protected, we might be able to do some good."

There was that word again. *We.* Whether she

liked it or not, they were bonded. "What about the baby?"

"It's a lot to think about." He dropped a light kiss on her forehead. "Time to get going if we're going to make it to Brewster's Pub by seven."

She desperately hoped that Jack Maddox would have some answers for them. She had absolutely no intention of spending the rest of her life on the run.

As THEY DROVE toward Rapid City, Drew gave Melinda a task to take her mind off the way her life had changed. "In the glove compartment, there are a couple of maps, including one for Rapid City. I want you to figure out a couple of escape routes for us."

"Actual paper maps?" Her eyebrows lifted. "That's so last century. Why can't I use the maps on the laptop?"

"I suppose you could, but—"

"Wait," she interrupted. "I know why. It's better if I don't turn on the laptop because, even if the bad guys don't know we're in this car, there might be a way of tracking our signal."

"You're sounding a little paranoid, Melinda."

"Don't you dare start teasing me."

He was glad to see that she'd gotten her spirit back. Her natural resilience impressed him. It seemed there was nothing he could throw at her that would keep her down.

"The reason for paper maps," he said, "is that they're easier than juggling a laptop if we're in a high speed chase. It's even better if you commit the maps to memory."

She bobbed her head. "I can do that. I'm pretty good at spatial relationships."

"You're good at everything." *Especially making love.* Knowing that she could self-heal made her even more attractive to him. She seemed to glow.

"I was thinking, Drew. Maybe we don't need to escape."

He didn't like the way that sounded. "How so?"

"I think we should take on the bad guys," she said. "There are two of us who can't be injured. We definitely have the edge."

"It's good that you've decided to embrace your abilities, but let's not get carried away."

"I mean it." She defiantly tossed her head. "We're indestructible. Why should we run?"

Time for a lesson. "As you've already seen for yourself, self-healing takes a toll. Afterward, you have a headache and you're exhausted."

"Afterward, we nap. First, we make a stand. Attack them before they attack us."

He never expected his little librarian to turn into a fiery avenger. "Let me explain a couple things. I've only had one injury that damaged an internal organ, and the healing process was rough. I don't want to risk being shot in the chest or the head."

"Theoretically, you—and I—should be able to heal any wound."

Long ago, he'd made a pact with himself. Though he'd been tempted to test his limits by firing a gun into his chest, he knew better than to abuse his abilities. He was certain that there were limits. "If the heart muscle is injured and the blood can't flow, I'm not sure what will happen."

"So we wear bullet-proof vests."

"Even if we're wearing body armor," he said, "there's another problem. And this is a big one."

She was listening intensely. "Tell me."

"When that guy broke in to your apartment, he caused you to black out. The whole time I was growing up, I had the same experience. I'm not sure how it's done. Probably not a drug because they wanted to run experiments with my blood. My best guess is that it's something electric, like a stun gun."

She sank back against the passenger seat. "They have some kind of weapon that knocks us out."

"Which is why we need to plan our escape."

With a crinkling of paper, she spread open the

maps from the glove compartment and started to study them. Though her aggressive streak seemed to be under control, he couldn't be sure of how she'd react when threatened. Working with a partner was new to him; he wouldn't feel safe until they were back at the cabin.

Chapter Twelve

At seven o'clock on a Friday night, Brewster's Pub in Rapid City was just beginning to come to life. Sports fans staked out seats nearest the television screens suspended over the bar in the middle of the long room. At the front tables, couples and groups chowed down on burgers and mountains of fries. In the back, a band was setting up on a small stage in front of a dance floor.

With an instinct born of years on the run, Drew took note of the exits. Swinging doors on the right side of the room led into the kitchen. Though he couldn't see the back wall, he assumed there was a door because the band was coming and going, carrying equipment.

Melinda poked him in the ribs. "Do you think I can get a burger?"

"Sure."

"Fries, too." A wide smile stretched her mouth. "I'm starved for decent comfort food."

She seemed calm, almost nonchalant. Either she was overconfident or unaware of the danger. Probably the latter. As they drove through Rapid City—a place he'd visited several times when he was a kid—they hadn't encountered anything resembling a threat. Hadn't even heard a police siren.

Melinda had done a good job of memorizing the maps. She'd recited street names as they approached and directed him to the pub on the far eastern side of town with nary a wrong turn. He'd parked under a cottonwood tree at the edge of the lot, ready for a quick escape.

A tall guy with short black hair sauntered toward them. He held out his hand. "I'm Jack."

Still uncertain about whether he could trust this guy, Drew introduced himself and Melinda. They followed Jack to a round wood table near the kitchen doors. Drew took the seat facing the entrance. When he sat, he adjusted the shoulder holster hidden under his leather jacket. He also wore an ankle holster.

Jack's companion was Claudia Reynolds, a pretty blonde with intelligent brown eyes. She defined her role. "I redesigned the eight-pointed star Web site."

"Claudia's a computer expert and Web designer." Jack's pride and affection were evident in his tone. "She's kind of a genius."

"Not a genius," she said modestly. "Kendra

Sinclair established the initial Web site with the eight-pointed star. She's a remarkable woman. Her ability is telekinesis."

"Really?" Melinda's eyes widened. "She can move things with her mind?"

Claudia nodded. "Hard to believe but true."

Drew asked, "Why did she use a star?"

"Kendra's father was an integral part of the experiments before he realized they were cruel and unethical. He imprinted all the subjects with a subconscious memory of the eight-pointed star. That's what led you to us."

"I'll be damned," he muttered.

"I have to compliment you, Drew. The encryption and firewalls on your computer are excellent. I couldn't trace your location."

"Good to know." But her comment worried him. Why had she tried to track him?

"There's a lot more you need to know." Jack rested his elbows on the table and leaned toward Drew. His eyes held the remote expression of someone accustomed to spending a lot of time alone, as though he was curious about the outside world and mistrustful of it at the same time. "Claudia put together a DVD with details. I'll give you the shorthand version."

"Are we in a hurry?" Melinda asked. "I'm dying for a burger and fries."

Drew shot her a glance. The woman was single-minded. He looked toward Jack and asked, "Is there any immediate danger?"

"I'm a pre-cog. Not a fortune teller. But there is one thing I can tell you. You're the subject of an all-out pursuit."

"Good guess."

Jack continued, "One of the people coming after you is a big, husky guy. If you've seen him, you'll remember. He's got a shaved head, like Kojak."

When Melinda gasped, Drew realized that he'd need to talk to her about not revealing too much. She wasn't good at keeping secrets.

"This big guy," she said. "What else do you know about him?"

"They call him Blue. There were three of them. Red, Blue and Green. Identical. The one called Red killed himself when we took him into custody."

"You arrested him?" Drew asked.

"Not exactly. I'm not a law officer. I was holding him for the FBI."

An interesting twist. "The Feds are involved in this investigation."

"They have been for years."

The waitress arrived with a tray holding a beer for Jack and a coffee for Claudia. Drew ordered burgers and fries for him and Melinda. She wanted an iced tea, and he went for the specialty-of-the-house dark beer. His self-healing blood meant he never got drunk or high, but he liked the taste.

To Jack, he said, "You mentioned something about giving me the short version."

"This started as a legitimate research project, funded by the military, to enhance individual skills and talents. In the experiments, they discovered a recessive gene, referred to as the I gene. 'I' stands for Ideal. Subjects who have this gene are affected when given certain drugs. They develop heightened abilities. The treatments work best when used on young people, before puberty. Therein was the problem."

Drew nodded. "Most people won't allow their children to be used as lab rats."

"The man in charge of these experiments is Kenneth Sykes."

Drew remembered the name he'd dredged from his subconscious and scribbled on a sheet of white paper. At some point in his life, he must have seen Sykes, but he didn't remember. "I assume that Sykes had to find children who were either orphaned or abandoned."

"And there were abductions." He tensed perceptibly. "My parents were killed when I was five. I blame Sykes."

Drew had never before made a connection between the death of his parents and the experiments. Horrified, he realized that the fatal plane crash that killed his mom and dad might have been part of the scheme.

Hiding his emotional response, he kept his voice level. "What happened to these children?"

"Sykes ran a lab, called The Facility, in the Black Hills. About two months ago, an undercover FBI agent infiltrated their operation, posing as a subject."

"What was his ability?" Melinda asked. "I assume he had one or he couldn't get inside."

"Telekinesis," Claudia said. "He has the same ability as Kendra. They're a couple now."

"Fancy that." Melinda cast a sidelong look in his direction. "They both had the same talent."

"Yeah, fancy that." Drew preferred playing his cards close to the vest. The less Jack and Claudia knew about them, the better. "Is The Facility still in operation?"

"The FBI closed it down. A real hellhole. You'll see photos on the DVD."

"What about Sykes?"

"Gone." Jack's voice was hollow. "There's evidence that he's working with foreign governments. They're the ones financing his operations. His current focus is developing the second generation, using the offspring of those with enhanced abilities."

Instead of blurting out that she was pregnant, Melinda grasped his hand under the table and squeezed hard. Her unspoken message was clear. *Sykes is after the baby. We have to protect our baby.*

Jack continued, "If you want protection, you can turn yourself in to the FBI."

A rational suggestion. But it held just about as much appeal as a life sentence in a super-max prison. "You haven't turned yourself in. Why not?"

"I need to be able to operate freely," Jack said. "My twin brother was at The Facility. He still hasn't been found."

"Oh, my gosh," Melinda whispered. "I'm so sorry."

"I won't quit," Jack said, "until I find him."

Apparently, he preferred to work without the constraints of the Feds. Drew completely understood. He'd never been good at following a chain of command or taking orders. All his life, he'd been a lone wolf.

Their food arrived. He knew Melinda had been shaken by Jack's information, and he watched her picking at her burger. When she straightened her shoulders, he knew she was giving herself an internal pep talk about bucking up and facing challenges. The practical thing would be to eat.

She grabbed the burger with two hands and took a huge bite. A trickle of juice ran down her lips, and she licked it off.

He loved her resilience.

His attitude was nowhere near as upbeat. When he thought of his parents' death being connected to some mysterious gene, his gut clenched in a painful knot. His life had been overturned by a genetic anomaly. He wouldn't let that happen to his child. They had to escape. But where could they run? If Sykes's men could track him down in Europe, they'd find him anywhere.

A shout rose from the bar where the television screens showed the college basketball games of March Madness.

"Got a favorite team?" Jack asked.

"I haven't followed it this year. I was out of the country."

"You're a freelance sports reporter, right?"

"Extreme sports," Drew said. "In Europe, I was covering glacier skiing and bicycle marathons."

"One of the guys with enhanced abilities has superspeed. I'd like to see him burn up a track. They say he can outrun a bullet."

Drew never would have believed him if it hadn't been for his own ability. "From what you've said, this Ideal gene operates differently in each individual."

"I don't understand how it works," Jack admitted. "But I can see why your ability is of particular interest to Sykes. What if he could reproduce this effect on a wider population? Develop an army of soldiers who could heal themselves?"

Drew was certain that he hadn't mentioned self-healing, and he didn't like Jack having information about him. "What else do you know about me?"

"You're the big fish that got away."

"I ran," Drew said.

"Changed your name half a dozen times," Jack said.

Melinda looked up from her burger. "What? Drew Kincaid isn't your real name?"

"It is now," he said.

"They've been looking for you," Jack said. "When The Facility closed down, they started putting out feelers. And they've been getting closer and closer."

"That's right," Drew said tersely.

"I need your help," Jack said. "Sykes is desperate to get his hands on you. We can use that to draw him into the open."

"You want to use me as bait."

Jack sipped his beer and set it down on the table. His motions were deliberate. "I wouldn't exactly put it that way. I'll arrange for backup so you're protected. But yes, I want to use you as bait."

Drew hadn't spent his entire adult life on the run only to hand himself over to his enemies, especially not now. Not with Melinda and a baby to consider.

Jack and his half-assed scheme could go to hell.

MELINDA KNEW THAT Drew wasn't comfortable with her behind the steering wheel of the Range Rover. But she'd pointed out that she'd memorized all the streets and knew the best way to get out of town, and he had acquiesced.

"We should do it," she said. "Jack and Claudia have the plan all figured out."

Drew growled, "I said I'd think about it."

He hadn't been real cooperative. Borderline rude, in fact.

Nevertheless, she hadn't given up on changing his mind. She turned off Main Street onto Sturgis Road, heading northwest toward the cabin. "We can't spend the rest of our lives on the run, Drew."

"Here's the problem with being bait," he said. "You can get chewed up and spit out before anybody has a chance to react."

"Sykes won't hurt you. He wants you alive."

"Not necessarily. He wants my self-healing ability. That's in my blood."

Their meeting with Jack and Claudia ended abruptly when Jack asked Drew if he'd give them a blood sample to analyze. To Melinda, it hadn't seemed like an unreasonable request, but Drew reacted with thinly veiled hostility. He'd glared as if Jack was a vampire, then he snarled something about how he didn't want to be anybody's experiment.

If she'd learned anything about Drew, it was that he was a loner and had been that way since he was a kid. All his report cards probably had the same notation: does not play well with others.

Somehow, she had to make him see reason. "I know it's hard for you to trust people. But this might be our best chance to end this mess."

"How do you figure?"

"You've been researching your past for years," she said. "And you didn't have any of the information Jack had about The Facility and Sykes and Blue, Green and Red."

"And the FBI," he said. "Don't forget the Feds."

"Is that what's bothering you? Are you afraid the FBI is going to take you into custody and do their own experiments?"

He fell silent, and she knew her guess was accurate. Though she couldn't claim to know what he was going through, she'd had a taste of that fear when she discovered she could self-heal.

And she was determined that their baby would not be victimized by a genetic fluke.

She drove past the lights and houses of Rapid City into the surrounding hills. The rugged terrain gave way to forests. She turned onto a twisting two-lane road that followed a narrow creek. Eventually, this route would circle back to a major thoroughfare, but she wanted a moment of solitude so they could talk without constantly scanning the approaching vehicles and watching for threats.

After a half mile without seeing anyone else on the road, she pulled onto the shoulder and parked.

"Tired of driving?" Drew asked hopefully.

"Not yet." She turned off the headlights and faced him, determined to make her point. "Things are changing for you. You're not the lone wolf anymore. You have me."

"Why did you stop here?"

"It seems like a relatively safe location. Nobody was following us. Nobody knows we're here."

In the moonlight, she saw him grin. "If you want to make love in the forest, I'm all for it. But I think we'd be safer near the cabin."

"This isn't about sex."

"Damn."

She was lying. Thoughts of making love to this incredible man were always running through her mind, but she had other concerns. "I need for you to trust me completely. There's no more need for secrets."

"I've told you everything."

"Not by a long shot. I don't even know your real name."

"David," he said. "David Andrew Barten."

She rested her hand on his cheek. "It's a nice name."

"But not who I am. Little Davey Barten was an orphan, a foster kid with a chip on his shoulder, a victim." He took her hand and pressed her palm against his lips. "I'm Drew Kincaid. A successful freelance journalist. A sportsman. An adult who determines his own fate."

Drew Kincaid was the man who had swept her off her feet, but there was a soft spot in her heart for the boy he once had been. In spite of his regenerative abilities, his childhood wounds had never healed.

"Jack gave you a warning," she said. "He's a precog. He can see things. And he said that you would need help, that you can't handle this by yourself."

"A handy bit of precognition," Drew said. "Jack wants me to sign on. It's to his advantage to have me cooperate. Would he have told me if he saw that his plan had any possibility of failure?"

"Wow, you're cynical." Jack Maddox didn't

come across as a scam artist or a con man. There was something deeply compelling about his ability, and Melinda believed him one hundred percent. "Jack isn't a liar."

"His primary focus is to rescue his twin brother. If anybody else—like me or you—gets hurt along the way, he might consider that to be an acceptable price."

"How can you say that? Jack and Claudia were nothing but helpful. They gave us a lot of information. And that DVD. And the secure cell phone to call them."

"Thanks for reminding me." He took the phone from his pocket. "This thing might put out a GPS tracking signal. I'm throwing it out the window."

"Don't you dare." She unfastened her seat belt and scrambled across the seats to snatch the cell phone from his hand. "They might need to contact us."

"I don't want to be contacted."

She was beginning to get seriously ticked off at him. "Why are you being so obstinate? Jack has access to information we don't know about, FBI information. He could alert us to danger."

"Maybe," he muttered.

"Finally! You're starting to listen to me."

When the phone in her hand rang, she

jumped. The caller ID read *unknown*. She flipped it open. "Hello?"

A man's voice said, "Put David on the phone."

She held the phone toward him. "He asked to speak to David."

"Tell him to go to hell."

She spoke into the phone. "I'm sorry, but—"

"Put me on speakerphone," the voice said.

She did as he asked. "You're on."

"Don't hang up. This is the FBI."

Drew glared at the phone. Anger radiated from him. His upper lip curled in disgust. "Hello, Daddy."

Chapter Thirteen

Drew took the phone from Melinda and switched off the speaker. His conversation with Harlan Anderson was sure to get ugly, and he didn't want her to hear. He pushed open the door to the Range Rover and stepped into the night. "How's Belle?"

"Don't know. We divorced years ago, not too long after you left town."

"How come?"

"We had our reasons."

Drew assumed that Harlan and Belle were complicit in the experiments. They conspired to keep him in the dark, telling him the blackouts were some kind of epilepsy, threatening him with being committed to an asylum. "Did Sykes pay you to keep me in the house close to The Facility?"

"Money changed hands," Harlan admitted. "But that's not why I did it. I was—"

"Stop. I don't need to hear your excuses."

There was no justification for what they'd done.

Anger wrenched Drew's gut. His muscles tensed, preparing for a fight. But there was no one to hit, nothing but a voice over the phone.

He strode along the shoulder of the road. Beside him, a rushing creek splashed over rocks and fallen branches. The cold night wind whistled through the tree branches.

"David? Are you still there?"

"Don't call me that. I'm Drew Kincaid."

"I've heard about your success." Harlan sneered on that last word. He'd always been stingy with praise.

"Success," Drew repeated. "They say it's the best revenge."

"I was the one who got you started with sports. Remember all those weekends when we watched baseball? And the basketball hoop in the driveway? We had some good times, son."

"I'm not your son."

"I protected you as best I could."

Drew recalled an echo of auditory memory when Harlan had been telling someone that he'd had enough. A feeble attempt at protection? "You lied to me."

"I had to. If we hadn't taken you in, you'd have been locked up in The Facility, caged like a wild animal. With me and Belle, you had a normal life."

His life had been a lot of things. Normal wasn't one of them. He'd always been different—an outsider, fearful of the blackouts, confused by his strange abilities. And angry, too. Angry, mostly. He lowered the phone from his ear, unable to listen to one more mendacious word without exploding.

In the forest on the opposite side of the creek, a twig snapped. Reacting swiftly, Drew pulled his Glock from the shoulder holster, dropped to one knee and aimed into the deep shadows between the rugged pine trees. A doe stepped out from behind a granite outcropping.

The sight of this gentle animal served as a reminder that unbridled rage wouldn't serve his purposes. He had to tamp down his anger. He shouldn't waste this opportunity to talk to the man who raised him.

"I've been looking for you, Harlan."

"Like you, I go by many names."

This conversation had started with a mention of the FBI, which made no sense to Drew. As far as he knew, Harlan was in sales for some kind of paper products company based in Washington, D.C., and he was on the road a lot. "You're a sales rep, right?"

"That was my cover." He paused. "I'm a federal agent. When you were living with us, I had other assignments, but my primary mission was to locate The Facility."

Drew took a moment to digest this information, unsure about whether or not he could believe Harlan. "I want verification."

"Not likely," Harlan said. "I can prove that I've been with the Bureau for over twenty years, but we don't give out details on undercover investigations."

"Let me get this straight. From the time I was ten until I was eighteen, you were trying to expose the place where these experiments were being conducted. Eight years. And you couldn't find the place."

"Sykes didn't put up road signs." His tone turned huffy and defensive. "I never knew when they'd take you. Sometimes, twice in a week. Other times, it would be a month or more. And if they knew I was following, we'd all be killed. Sykes was never shy about letting me know who was in control."

"What about satellite imaging? Aerial photographs? What about a good old-fashioned search with a couple of dozen agents?"

"We couldn't risk it."

Or maybe the FBI didn't want to take that risk. Maybe they were interested in seeing how the experiments turned out. Maybe they wanted his self-healing ability. "The Feds knew what was happening to me, and they allowed it to continue."

"There were other people involved—innocent

victims being held in The Facility. We couldn't risk their lives. Hey, I didn't come up with the game plan. I was just following orders."

Just following orders. How many atrocities had been perpetrated with that excuse? Drew said, "I heard that The Facility was raided a couple of months ago."

"Yeah, and look how that turned out. Not good. Sykes got away with all his research. He took off like a Sammy Sosa home run hit over the center field fence. There's only one way to find him now. And that requires your cooperation."

Drew pivoted on the road and started back toward the Range Rover. Melinda leaned against the front bumper with her arms folded below her breasts. Moonlight caught in her curly hair, outlining her face like a halo.

He knew that she'd want him to cooperate with the FBI. To play nice. She trusted that these people who had allowed him to be victimized would do the right thing.

"There's one thing I need to know," Drew said. "The death of my parents. Was it an accident?"

"We don't know." He exhaled a sigh into the phone. "Military medical records showed that your father had the I gene. That's why you were considered a good candidate for the experiments."

"I need an answer," Drew said harshly.

"Your parents went down in a small plane. It looked like wind shear was the problem. The FAA found no evidence of sabotage."

"Damn it, Harlan. Tell me."

"I don't know."

Drew's fingers clenched around the cell phone. The glow from the screen mocked him in the darkness. He wanted to smash it with a rock. If it had been up to him, he'd say the hell with this. He'd climb into the vehicle and drive until he disappeared into the unknown. But he had Melinda and the baby to think about. "What do you want from me?"

"Give me a chance to explain. Tell me where you are. I'll meet with you."

As if he'd trust this man? "I'm not giving you my location."

"Okay, how about if we meet tomorrow. At the old house in Lead."

"I'll think about it."

"No matter what you believe, I've always cared about you. Let me make things right. Tomorrow. If you can't make it at noon, I'll wait."

Drew ended the call. As he approached the Range Rover, Melinda came toward him. Even in the dim moonlight, he could see the worry on her face, and he was deeply sorry for dragging her into the disaster that was his life. He should have known better than to get involved with her, should have left her alone.

He held out the cell phone, keeping her at arm's length. "Take the damn phone. I'm done talking."

Ignoring him, she came closer. Her hands slipped inside his jacket as her arms encircled him. She adjusted her position to accommodate the shoulder holster. Her head nestled in the crook of his neck. Softly, she murmured, "It's okay, Drew. We're going to get through this."

"How the hell can you know?" He heard the brusque rejection in his voice. His arms were straight at his sides, refusing to embrace her. Sex was one thing—one very good thing. But he wasn't a fan of affection. "What are you doing?"

Her head tilted back and she looked up at him. "I'm comforting you, letting you know that I care."

"I don't need comfort."

"But you do." She didn't seem to be arguing, just stating a fact. "You're so furious that you almost mowed down an innocent deer in the forest. And you have every right to be angry after what you've been through."

"What's the point of being comforted?"

"It's not a reasoned response. It's a gift," she said. "Open your arms and accept it. Accept me."

He couldn't say no. He wrapped his arms around her and held on tight.

MELINDA'S MOM always said you couldn't understand another person until you walked a mile in their shoes. Though Melinda had only taken a couple of baby steps with Drew's self-healing ability, she was already overwhelmed. The ability wasn't actually the issue. It was everything that went with it. The espionage. The pursuit. The danger.

She was certain that they needed help to navigate through these obstacles.

After some intense talking, she'd convinced Drew to return to Rapid City to see Jack and Claudia again. Following their directions, she drove to the Quiet Valley Motel. A neon sign on the front office said Vacancy. The parking lot was circular. In the center was a fenced pond, a couple of ragged pine trees and a replica of Mount Rushmore. The rooms were separate cabins. Claudia said they were in number eight. A reference to the eight-pointed star?

As Melinda parked, she looked over at Drew. He'd been awfully quiet since his phone call with Harlan, and she feared that he was reliving memories of his younger days. "Thinking of Harlan?"

"He wasn't a bad father," Drew said. "Kind of distant. Not home very often. But he didn't slap me around or anything."

"He wasn't a father. Never intended to be," she

said. "Like he told you, he was doing his job as an FBI agent, and that didn't include being a parent. He was a caretaker."

His gaze met hers. "What's the difference?"

"You'll know," she said with confidence. "When our baby is born, you'll know what it means to be a dad."

"I'm glad you think so," he said as he opened the car door.

Though Drew never had a decent male role model, she was certain he had the capacity to love. In spite of everything, he was a good person, capable of empathy. That was one reason he was so good at writing interviews. When they first started dating, she'd read some of his articles, and she appreciated the depth his words gave to a goofball skateboarder or a world-class cyclist in the Tour de France.

Jack opened the door to number eight before they knocked, which she figured was a pre-cog thing. A little disconcerting.

Drew confronted him immediately. "Why the hell did you give the cell phone number to Harlan?"

"I wanted to convince you that we're legitimate, working with the FBI."

"He's the worst possible messenger you could send. I don't trust Harlan."

Still, Drew walked through the door into the cabin, and Melinda followed. She had to wonder if Jack's pre-cog ability had told him this would be the outcome after Harlan's phone call.

The interior of the cabin was narrow, only a little more than twenty feet across, and they had to dodge between a bed and a sleeper sofa to get to a round kitchen table in front of a half-wall divider that separated them from a kitchenette.

Claudia rose from the table where she'd been on the computer. "No need for worry. We're safe here."

"How do you know?" Drew demanded.

"Well, there's Jack," she said with a fond smile in his direction. "He doesn't foresee any threat. And I've also set up surveillance scans."

Drew went toward her, obviously interested in any sort of security technology. "Show me what you've got."

Melinda turned to Jack. "Is Harlan a safe contact?"

"It's hard to get a good read on him. He specializes in undercover work. Duality is his nature, which makes it hard to know where his true loyalty lies. But we need him. He's our contact for reaching Sykes."

"He asked Drew to meet him tomorrow at noon at the house where they used to live in Lead."

"We can arrange to follow him and have other agents present in case Harlan tries to pull something." Jack frowned. "I have a sense that there's something bad about that house, something Harlan doesn't want us to know."

"Like what?"

"Something from the past. Something dangerous."

Oh, swell. Another threat. The risks were piling up around them like kindling for a bonfire. "Are there precautions we can take?"

"There's one." He went toward the table where Drew and Claudia were poring over a rectangular electronic object. "I'd like for you both to have a GPS chip implanted. That way we can track you."

Drew scowled. "GPS would show you the location of my cabin. That's something I want to keep secret."

Melinda assured him, "Of course, we trust you, but—"

"I understand," Claudia said as she reached for a briefcase, which she placed on the table and opened. "I'd have the only receiver. Nobody else could follow you."

"What kind of range are we talking about?" he asked.

"Thousands of miles with pinpoint accuracy." She gave him a smug grin. "This is top-of-the-line FBI equipment."

"But the Feds can't trace the signal?"

"Not without the receiver."

He still looked hesitant, so Melinda stepped up. "I'll do it. I like the idea of having someone know where I am."

"Roll up your sleeve," Claudia said as she took an injection device from the briefcase. "I'll zap this tiny chip under your skin. It barely hurts at all. If we need to find you, we can activate the transmitter. Otherwise, I won't turn it on."

Melinda took off her jacket and tossed it on the bed. She pushed her sweater sleeve up on her arm. Before she could present her arm to Claudia, Drew caught hold of her hand and turned her toward him. "Are you sure about this?"

"I want every advantage I can get."

"Your decision affects me," he said. "If you're on the grid, it means I am, too."

"Not if you aren't with me."

As she spoke, she realized that she was forcing him to make a choice. Either he could continue by himself or he could commit himself to staying with her, even if it meant doing something he didn't want to do.

She wanted him to choose her. If he turned his back and stormed out the door, she didn't know if she could stop herself from running after him.

He leaned close and whispered in her ear, "I'll never leave you, Melinda."

Stepping back, he peeled off his jacket, revealing the shoulder holster. "Might as well zap me, too."

Claudia implanted the chips. First in Melinda, then in Drew. "While you've got your sleeve up," she said, "I'd like to take a blood sample."

Earlier tonight, Drew had nearly erupted at the suggestion of drawing his blood. Now, he merely shrugged. "Let's do it."

Melinda sat beside him at the table, smiling into his eyes. His willingness to cooperate pleased her; it was a step toward realizing that he wasn't all alone in the world. There were people he could trust. "What changed your mind?"

"Something you said earlier. About my blood being used to cure disease."

Though it sounded good, she didn't quite believe that his motives were utterly altruistic. "And?"

"Sykes turned me into a freak for his own selfish motives. If my ability can be used for good, it's revenge."

Jack stood beside him. "There won't be experiments using your blood," he promised. "I've had it done to me. I know what it's like."

"Good," Drew said. "I don't want to provide transfusions for the FBI, not after what Harlan did."

Melinda wondered if her blood would also be useful. Though she'd self-healed her injuries after her fall, she probably wasn't full-strength like Drew. And she worried about possible effects on the baby.

Jack gave her shoulder a reassuring pat. "It's okay. We don't need your blood."

She exchanged a look with Drew. They hadn't mentioned her enhanced ability, hadn't told them about her pregnancy.

"We know," Claudia said with a warm smile. "Congratulations."

"You're carrying the second generation," Jack said. "And the baby has inherited the self-healing characteristic."

"Yes," she said.

"I'm afraid that makes you a prized target," Jack said. "Sykes might want you even more than he wants Drew."

"Not me," she said with dark awareness. "He wants my baby."

Chapter Fourteen

As they drove back toward the cabin, Melinda noticed a shift in Drew's mood. Though he continued his vigilance, as he scanned the roads and checked the rearview mirrors, he seemed almost lighthearted. After he'd made his decision to be part of the team, the weight of life-and-death responsibility lifted, and he transformed into the charming guy who attracted her in the first place. He made her laugh and entertained her with stories of his extreme-sporting exploits that didn't seem nearly so dangerous now that she knew he could heal himself.

They were nearing the final turn when she said, "You've talked about skiing and car racing and motocross. What about riding horses? Have you ever done rodeo?"

"I grew up in the Black Hills, but I'm a city guy. I like sports that go fast."

"Not a fan of bull riding?"

"I'm always a fan," he said. "I like watching any athlete perform. But I never got into rodeo. I'm better at riding motorcycles than horses."

"Like the motorcycle in the garage at the cabin?"

He shot her a grin. "Tomorrow we'll take it out."

His mention of tomorrow's plans reminded her. "Did you want to take the motorcycle to meet Harlan?"

"Maybe." He guided the Range Rover down the near-invisible trail through the trees that led to the cabin. "You haven't talked about your favorite sports."

"Not much to say. Being from Minnesota means I've seen a lot of hockey. And I'm a Vikings fan, of course. And I once dated a college football player for the Gophers."

"The Gophers." He nudged her arm. "There's a team name that strikes terror into the hearts of their opponents."

"For your information, gophers can be really mean when they're not digging tunnels through your backyard."

"Fearsome rodents." He parked in front of the cabin. "I'll let you out here with the supplies while I put the car away. The garage is pretty cramped."

She opened her door and hopped out. After they

unloaded four grocery bags with enough fresh vegetables and meat to avoid his stash of bomb shelter cuisine for a few days, she went to the porch. Taking the cell phone from her purse, she turned it on. They might need to be in contact with Jack and Claudia, and she wasn't sure they'd get a signal in this secluded forest hideaway.

To her relief, the phone was fully charged and seemed to be working. There was one missed call. Jack and Claudia? Though tempted to hit redial, she was aware that there were tracking issues. Claudia had assured her that this phone had no GPS chip, but the signal could be triangulated. She turned off the phone.

When Drew approached, she held it up. "I turned this on. Just for a second. We missed a call."

"Harlan has that cell phone number," he said. "Let's leave it turned off. Later, I'll contact Jack and Claudia on the computer."

She nodded. Drew's computer was, as Claudia assured them, untraceable. "Why wait until later?"

"There's something more urgent." He unlocked the door and pushed it open. "A pressing need."

With a rising sense of apprehension, she followed him into the cabin. Was there some danger he hadn't told her about? Some new and terrible threat? She waited impatiently while he activated the computer and the camera surveillance systems. "What is it, Drew? Are we safe?"

He swept her into his arms. "The only one who's going to attack you tonight is me."

His erection was hard against her belly. "Is this the pressing need you were talking about?"

"There's nothing more urgent than making love to you."

"Nothing?"

"Not right now."

She rubbed against him, arching her back as she gazed into his dark green eyes. The winter clothing separating them felt as heavy as armor. She was ready to throw off her jacket and all the other layers in a frenzy, but Drew seemed to have another idea. He reached back and touched a couple of keys on the computer. Soft jazz with a sexy saxophone drifted through the speakers in subtle accompaniment. He held her, and they swayed together. His hands slipped rhythmically over her body as he removed her jacket.

He cupped her face gently, but his mouth was hard and demanding against hers. His thorough kiss left her breathless and a little bit dazed. Flickers of pure energy danced in her peripheral vision as he peeled off her sweater and reached for the button on her waistband. Slowly, in time to the jazz beat, he eased her jeans below her hips.

That was where she stopped him. Melinda wanted to be involved in this jazzy striptease. She wanted his clothes gone. First, the jacket.

"The holster." Her fingers plucked at the thick canvas straps. "Take it off."

"You don't want me to wear my Glock?"

Fumbling with the holster, she suddenly had great sympathy for teenaged boys struggling to unfasten their girlfriend's brassieres. "Get rid of the holster or I'll tell you what you can do with your Glock."

"Tough talk for a librarian."

But he helped her with the holster. In minutes, he had bared his chest. Her own shirt and bra followed. Naked from the waist up, they joined together. The mingled warmth of their bodies heated up the cabin. She loved touching him, savoring his muscular body.

With Drew, she felt no hesitation. He encouraged her with light strokes that sent shivers across her flesh. Though they were both trying to go slow and prolong the pleasure, their need was too great.

They tore off the last bits of clothing. He lowered her to the mattress, holding and kissing her at the same time, which was a rather impressive feat of coordination. A skilled lover, he was far more experienced than she was. He directed, and she responded with enthusiasm. And passionate bursts of her own creativity.

Catching him off guard, she flipped positions so she was on top. He seemed surprised and pleased at the same time. She rose above him, straddling him, then lowered herself, taking him inside her inch by inch.

He reached for her, but she held him down as she rotated her hips in a slow circle. Tremors raced through her body as she moved faster, with more *urgency*. When she began to crumble in orgasm, he took charge.

Their positions reversed. Though she was already gasping, he drove hard into her, sparking another set of wild thrills. The pleasure went far beyond anything she'd ever imagined.

After he released his supersperm and collapsed on the mattress beside her, she didn't know if she'd ever be able to move again. And she didn't particularly want to. She'd be content to lie here, wallowing in bliss.

He propped himself up on an elbow and gazed down at her. "How did a librarian get to be so good in bed?"

"I've read the *Kama Sutra*."

"Any special positions you'd like to try?"

"Not right now." She smiled at him. "I'm spent."

He kissed the tip of her nose. "You rest. I'll put away the groceries."

She loved that he didn't feel the need for clothing as he did the simple housekeeping chores. As he went back and forth to the kitchen area, there was a strut in his step. His body was gorgeous from every angle. She sighed and said, "I love this cabin."

"Don't get too attached to it."

"Why not? Are you going to blow it up?"

He grinned. "If necessary."

"That's not funny, Drew."

He brought her a bottled water, uncapped it and held it to her lips. She tasted a sip, then lay back, waiting for him to join her.

Instead, he slipped into his jeans and he went to the computer. Though she was too blissed out to complain, she would have enjoyed a bit of cuddle time. "What are you doing?"

"No need for you to move a muscle. I thought I'd check out the DVD Jack and Claudia gave us. I'm curious about The Facility."

She rolled over and buried her face in the pillow, wishing she could do the normal thing—relax in her lover's arms. Instead of holding her, he seemed determined to open a whole new box of trouble.

DREW BELIEVED in research. The more he knew, the better prepared he'd be. That had been his logical rationale for cooperating with Jack and Claudia. They had connections that gave them access to better resources.

By reviewing the information on the DVD, he hoped to trigger his buried memories as well as adding to his knowledge about The Facility. He turned the volume low so he wouldn't disturb Melinda as he watched.

The eight-pointed star filled the computer screen as Claudia narrated, giving a brief history of genetic experiments designed to enhance natural abilities.

The thesis sounded innocent enough, maybe even scientifically admirable. Then, they discovered the I gene, which could be supercharged.

Initially, Sykes had a research partner, Benjamin Stewart, who had ethical concerns about their project from the very start. Without telling Sykes, Stewart wrote secret codes into the genes. One of these codes created a subliminal memory of the eight-pointed star that could be used to link the subjects of the experiments.

Claudia had used that memory on the Web site to contact research subjects.

Drew was aware that Melinda had left the mattress. Wrapped in one of the sleeping bags like a giant cocoon, she peeked over his shoulder.

He hit Pause and turned toward her. "I thought you were tired."

"This is interesting. Do you think the baby will remember that star?"

"It won't be necessary." He pulled her around so she was sitting on his lap. "We're going to end this threat. Our child won't have to give a second thought to Sykes or experiments or any of this."

As she shifted around on his lap, he felt like he was wrestling with a giant stuffed animal.

"The sleeping bag isn't working for me," she said.

She shuffled across the floor to her suitcase. When she bent down to root through her clothes, the sleeping bag fell from her shoulders. He watched as gradually her naked body was revealed. The curve of her slender waist flared into her hips and her ripe, full buttocks. Damn, she was pretty. He was tempted to turn off the DVD and make love to her again.

After slipping a nightshirt over her head, she came back toward him with a prim librarian smile lifting the corners of her wide mouth. She settled easily on his lap. "Start it up."

As Claudia's narration continued, a series of still photos showed a standard-looking laboratory. She talked more about Stewart. He'd died in an accident that was probably murder. With Sykes in charge, there were no ethical boundaries. Experimentation on young subjects produced better results, and the researchers were on the lookout for kids with the I gene. When these children were located, Sykes went to great lengths to recruit them. Claudia cited the example of Jack and his twin brother, who came to The Facility after the suspicious death of their parents.

This time it was Melinda who hit Pause. "Do you think Sykes killed your mom and dad?"

"I'll never know for sure."

"I don't think Sykes was involved in their death."

"Why not?"

She rested her hand on his cheek. Her touch felt cool and soothing. "Sykes didn't grab you immediately after they died. You bounced around in foster care for several years. If he arranged their accident to get to you, it seems like he would have scooped you into his net right away."

"Like he did with Jack and his twin."

Drew never thought he'd be glad about the time he spent in foster care, but he was pleased to latch on to a theory that meant the death of his parents wasn't his fault.

He started the DVD again. The screen was filled with a series of photographs of a small, slight man with dark eyes and wild hair. In many of the pictures he wore a lab coat. In others, he had on a rumpled suit. These photos showed an age progression, from messy brown hair to wiry, tangled, white locks. It was Sykes.

Drew remembered that face in many incarnations. He'd been acquainted with the younger Sykes at the lab. The memory struck a physical chord. He remembered constraints, being unable to move while he was poked and prodded. And needles that pierced his skin. His skin prickled as he remembered an unbearable fear.

He paused on a full-length shot of Sykes. His white hair looked like he'd stuck his finger in an electrical socket. His necktie was lopsided. His fists thrust deep into the pockets of his trousers.

Drew recognized that posture. Sykes was the man he'd seen on the Amalfi cliffs in Italy. Sykes had been standing beside the man called Blue. "He was after me in Europe."

Melinda twisted around to look into his eyes. "You saw him?"

"I didn't know who he was, but he looked familiar." If Drew hadn't been so focused on escape, he could have confronted Sykes. "I let him get away."

"Don't blame yourself," she said. "You played it smart. You evaded capture."

"My days of being on the run are over. I'm going to end this thing."

The next section on the DVD started with a road map showing the location of The Facility. Another map followed; this one showed the natural terrain. Rugged cliffs. Thick forests. A narrow creek that flowed from a kidney-shaped lake. The picture switched to a handheld camera focused through a windshield. The twisting mountain roads looked like thousands of other routes through the Black Hills. The person holding the camera left the vehicle and walked on a path. Behind a towering granite stone was the entrance to a limestone cave.

"Impressive secrecy," Drew said. "Aerial photos wouldn't have shown this location."

The camera turned in a circle, recording the surroundings. He hit Pause and pointed. "Do you see that little shack? By those other rocks?"

"It doesn't look much bigger than an outhouse."

"Sentries could be posted there. If anybody happened to stumble into the area, they'd be turned back."

"Or shot," she said. "Harlan might have been telling the truth when he said he couldn't find the place."

But Drew wasn't about to let his foster father off the hook. "He had eight years, and the map shows The Facility wasn't far from Lead. Harlan couldn't find The Facility because he was scared."

Melinda shuddered. "So am I."

He couldn't honestly tell her that there was

nothing to fear. Great evil had taken place inside The Facility.

When the camera entered the cave, the picture wasn't entirely clear. It looked as if there were barracks, several structures. The interior of one had been a laboratory with long counters and sinks. Another was a ransacked office with file drawers hanging open. One was referred to as "the morgue," but the camera didn't go there. The examination rooms were shells, devoid of equipment. Some of the housing was dormitory style, fairly comfortable. Other spaces were cages, barred jail cells.

"Terrible," Melinda whispered. "Why would children have to be locked up?"

"They had abilities. They might have been dangerous."

Had he been locked up in that dark cave? He couldn't remember, and maybe it was better that he didn't have a clear recollection.

The rest of the DVD showed mug shots of various scientists and lab technicians, suspected of being involved with Sykes. An unfocused photo of a man with a shaved head could have been one of the three—Red, Blue or Green.

Next, there were photos of people who had been subjects of the experiments, each with a brief biography. The first was Jack Maddox. Next was Matt Whitlock, a rangy guy in a cowboy hat who had the ability to manipulate thought. A businessman named Kane Black was capable of superspeed. Zack O'Hara, the undercover FBI agent who had located The Facility, was telekinetic.

There were others with abilities. Other victims.

Melinda snuggled against his chest. Her body molded against him. "This is an impressive group. Looking at all these people with their special talents, I can almost understand why these experiments were undertaken."

His arm snaked around her rib cage, and he pulled her close. "It started off as a good plan."

"Then turned evil." She turned her head to kiss his jaw. "If someone had told you that you could have the ability to heal yourself, would you have volunteered?"

"The experiments started when I was ten," he reminded her. "Too young to make that kind of life-changing decision."

"And now?"

If he had his life to do over, he'd make changes, starting with keeping his parents alive. His years on the run, always looking over his shoulder, had been hell. But he'd done okay. "There's one thing I wouldn't have done differently."

"What's that?"

"Following the path that led me to you." His

hand slid lower and stroked her belly. "Making a baby with you."

She purred and snuggled closer. "I like that, too."

"Tomorrow morning," he said, "I want to go there. To The Facility."

"Why?"

He needed to see for himself, to fully understand and accept what had happened to him. He needed to remember. There might be a clue, a buried memory stuck inside his head that could lead to Sykes.

Chapter Fifteen

The next morning, after a decent breakfast of sausage and eggs, they headed out to the garage. Drew had already decided the Harley would be best for this off-road journey to The Facility.

"Are you sure we should do this?" Melinda asked. "It seems to me that we ought to coordinate with Jack and Claudia."

"We can do both." Though he'd agreed to cooperate, he'd been his own man for too long to start checking in before he made a move. "You have the cell phone. When we're at The Facility, we'll call Jack."

If they were late to meet Harlan at noon, that was just too damn bad. The old man said he'd wait. Drew moved the Range Rover so there would be room to get the bike through the garage door. He pulled the cover off the Harley—a fine machine. As he wheeled it out of the garage, sunshine reflected off the chrome fender and sparkled on the headlight.

"There's only one helmet." He held it toward Melinda. Despite her ability to self-heal, he wanted to protect her.

Gamely, she put it on. "Nice bike."

"More than nice," he said. "I adapted this baby from a lightweight dirt-bike frame. The engine is V-Twin with full power. Retooled suspension, dual exhaust, antilock brakes. It has maneuverability and power."

She didn't seem impressed. "Just be careful. Safety first, Drew."

"If you're worried, you should stay here at the cabin," he suggested as he mounted the bike. "Then you could e-mail back and forth with Jack and Claudia."

"I'm coming with you." She climbed on behind him. "You need me."

He cranked the engine and was answered with a satisfying roar—a primal rumble. There was nothing better than going fast on a bike, feeling the wind, eating up the road.

Her arms wrapped snugly around him as he took off. He'd studied the maps on the DVD and printed one of them out. In terms of distance, they weren't far from Lead or from The Facility. The trick would be to successfully chart his course through all these winding mountain roads. The route became increasingly familiar as they neared the area where he grew up. He'd traveled this way before.

Drew had never had a car of his own, but Harlan had let him drive the family station wagon on occasion. He had never been allowed to take the car when his foster father was out of town, not even to run errands for Belle.

They'd kept him on a short leash, limited in his range of movement. One of the few times he was allowed to see the wider world was that trip to the lake near Pierre with Harlan.

His desperate escape to New York City must have stunned Harlan. Drew smiled to himself. They never expected him to run so far, never thought he'd be able to find his way.

The final turnoff to The Facility had recently been traveled. Tire ruts dug into the dirt road. The bare branches of low foliage had been crushed and broken.

Proceeding slowly on the bike, he watching for the natural landmarks he'd seen on the DVD.

Melinda tapped his shoulder and pointed to a high spot on the cliff. "Over there. The sentry house."

The weathered wood blended into the surrounding trees. "Good eye."

At a fork in the road, he went left. They were close enough. He rounded the last boulder on the road and saw the entrance to the limestone cave. The opening was surprisingly large. Though he could have driven inside, he parked the bike at the side of the road. In the wind, he heard the sighs of victims. This was the place.

Melinda groaned as she dismounted. "Oh, my gosh, my legs feel like jelly."

"In a couple of minutes, you'll be fine."

She pulled off the helmet. "How do you know?"

"It's a self-healing thing. If you're like me—"

"And I am," she asserted.

"Your blood is constantly regenerating and repairing. It doesn't make you a better athlete, but you'll find that your stamina is much improved."

"Bonus." A wide grin spread across her face. "Self-healing is going to be real helpful with my jogging regimen. I might even go back to that spinning class at the gym where that pushy instructor was always yelling, 'Five more minutes—you can do it.' Ha! I'll show her five more minutes."

He was glad to have her with him. Entering this cave could trigger memories of the worst trauma in his life, and he trusted Melinda to keep him grounded.

As she fluffed her hair into shape, she asked, "Do you remember anything?"

His only impressions were vague and fuzzy. "I think I was carried, brought into the cave on a gurney."

He'd thought far enough ahead to bring a couple of high-beam flashlights. He gave one to Melinda and kept one for himself. Stepping into the darkness, he turned on the light. Inside the high, arched walls of the cave were low buildings—an underground city that looked like army barracks.

Though he'd hoped that memories would come flooding back, Drew felt nothing. Not even a twinge. All he could do was marvel at the cleverness of this hideout. The Facility made his secure cabin look like a pathetic attempt at secrecy. No one could find them here; Sykes had operated for years and years without notice.

After only a few paces, he heard a noise but wasn't sure where it was coming from. The cave walls amplified and echoed every sound.

He paused and signaled for Melinda to do the same. They stood very still. Listening.

When he heard it again, he turned the flashlight to the right. The big man with the shaved head charged toward them. He held something in his hand.

They couldn't take a chance on being thrown into a blackout. There wasn't time to pull his gun from the holster. Not a second to lose. "Run."

FIGHT OR FLIGHT? No question in Melinda's mind. It was time to run. She pivoted on her heel and dashed toward the sunlight outside the cave where the Harley awaited.

Behind her, Drew had taken his gun from the shoulder holster. He fired two shots into the maw of the cave. Before she reached the trees where the motorcycle was parked, he yelled, "Not the bike. Melinda, over there. Take that path."

Zipping away on the Harley had seemed like the most logical escape, but she didn't question his order. Drew had been on the run for years. He knew best.

She ran as fast as she could. Twigs brushed against her jeans as she followed the rocky path downhill toward a trickling stream, narrow enough that she could jump across if needed. Not that she intended to try any tricky maneuvers. The uneven footing on the path made it hard enough to keep from falling flat on her face.

Her jogging routes in Sioux Falls were flat, and the biggest obstacle was an uneven piece of sidewalk. This was mountain wilderness, untamed. The path widened into a clearing with other branches shooting off in different directions. "Which way?" she yelled.

"Downhill," he said. "Keep going downhill."

Gunfire sounded behind her. Drew told her

he'd never been shot. What would happen if he was hit by a bullet? Even if he healed, he'd be momentarily helpless. Did he have another gun she could use? Could she drag him to safety?

She dodged around a clump of trees that separated her from the creek. Though Drew said run downhill, there was no way to go but up. Her toes dug into the gravelly soil as she climbed. Her foot slipped. She fell, whacked her knee on a rock. A jolt of pain shot through her leg. *I'll heal.* She scrambled to her feet and kept going.

The tree trunks were farther apart. She emerged onto a sloping cliff. In the distance, through tangled pine boughs, she saw the shimmer of sunlight on a lake.

"Keep going," Drew shouted.

Sidestepping down the rugged slope, she couldn't avoid putting weight on her injured leg. Instead of hurting more, the pain lessened. At the bottom of the slope, Drew grasped her arm and pulled her behind the cover of a boulder.

Breathing hard, she asked, "Why didn't we take the bike?"

"We could be riding into an ambush. I don't know if Blue is acting alone."

There could be more of them. Fear clenched her lungs. She couldn't breathe.

Drew replaced the ammunition clip in his gun.

"I don't want anybody to get close enough to trigger a blackout."

"Oh, gosh." She gasped. "How are we going to get away?"

He held her face. His hand was steady. His eyes shone with determination. "Work with me, Melinda."

Easy for him to say; he was a daredevil. Risk didn't scare him. "What, what, what? What can I do?"

"Use the cell phone. Call Jack and Claudia. Tell them to activate the GPS chips."

Though his instructions were clear, her brain took a moment to sort out what he meant. The cell phone? The chip?

Another shot rang out. Drew peeked over the top of the boulder and returned fire.

She took the cell phone from her jacket pocket. It seemed to take forever to turn on, but when it did, she was in luck. She had reception. When she hit the automatic dial, Claudia answered right away.

"We're in trouble," Melinda said into the phone. "We need help."

"Where are you?"

"I don't know. A forest. There's a lake." Her gaze scanned the surrounding forests and craggy hillsides. How could she possibly give directions?

More important, how could Claudia and Jack get here in time? Their motel in Rapid City was over an hour away. "Where are you?"

"On the road. We thought we'd go toward Lead and check out the location where Drew is supposed to meet with Harlan."

Melinda couldn't think, couldn't concentrate. Someone was shooting at them. The man with the shaved head. Blue. "Claudia, hurry. Activate the GPS chips."

"Got it," Claudia said. "Try to get to a road where we can pick you up."

She disconnected the call.

Drew faced her with his back against the rock. "Take off your jacket."

Though she did as he said, she asked, "Why?"

"This is my last clip. I've only got about five shots left so we can't stay here and make a stand."

"What does that mean?"

"We run. Down the hill to that lake. The water is runoff from melted snow. Too cold for them to follow us."

He wanted her to dive into a freezing-cold mountain lake? "Oh, boy."

"Problem?" He set down the gun to peel off his leather jacket. "You know how to swim, don't you?"

"Well, sure. But isn't there another way?"

"Trust me, baby."

He gave her a wink, which she thought was carrying the macho image a bit too far. Clearly, the man didn't have the good sense to be scared when he was in mortal danger.

He peeked around the edge of the rock. "I'm going to start shooting. That should provide some cover. You take off for the lake. I'll be right behind you."

He poked his head out and opened fire. With gunshots ringing in her ears, she dashed down the hill and ducked into the trees. With no path to follow, she dodged through a maze of pine trunks. Her level of exertion was intense, but her legs had strength. The injury to her knee had faded to a light stinging sensation. She ducked under a limb, jumped over a fallen log. *Keep going.*

She didn't dare look back over her shoulder, didn't want to know how close Blue was to catching them. Her only focus was racing downhill toward the lake.

Drew pulled even with her. Running hard, he shoved through branches with his gun still in hand. "You can do it, Melinda."

As if I have a choice? She heard a gunshot and cringed. Her back prickled as she imagined the bullet tearing through her flesh.

Then she saw the water—a tranquil blue

expanse at the edge of the trees. Golly, it was going to be cold. In summertime, the lakes warmed up enough for swimming, especially around Rapid City. But this was the end of winter in the mountains.

Coming out of the forest, there was about three feet of rocks and sand leading to the edge of the lake. Instinctively, she hesitated.

Drew caught hold of her hand and pulled her. She took the plunge.

Chapter Sixteen

Water splashed around his thighs as Drew pulled her into the lake with him. The cold took his breath away. Each icy drop stung like a tiny needle, piercing his nervous system. Waist-deep, he glided along the surface and ducked his head under the water.

Melinda did the same. He'd been proud of her speed and agility when she was running. Now, she proved herself again. Without a single complaint, she stretched out, kicked with her legs and went into a crawl stroke, which was pretty damned impressive given that they were both fully dressed and wearing shoes.

Though he could have propelled himself through the water at greater speed, he stayed at her side. Flipping to his back, he surveyed the shoreline. They were already a good fifty yards away from the trees. No sign of Blue. Not yet.

"Keep going," he encouraged her. "You're doing great."

She sputtered an unintelligible response and kept stroking. She was a good woman, strong and resilient. He swore to get her through this in one piece. Melinda and the baby would survive no matter what. His own safety was secondary.

His teeth began to chatter, and he clenched his jaw. He needed a plan.

The mountain lake was small and shaped like the letter *B*. If he remembered correctly from the map, it fed into a creek that was wide enough to be named. Piney Creek? Spiny Creek? He couldn't see the topography while in the water, but he directed her toward the spit of land that thrust into the lake at the middle.

If they climbed out at that point, they could make a run from there. It would take Blue a long time to get around the lake, unless he had a dirt bike.

The cold seeped into his bones, and the weight of his clothing dragged him down. Pulling through the frigid water took an effort. If they got all the way to the other side of the lake, they'd have a more significant lead.

This time, when he looked back toward shore, he spotted Blue's shaved head. There was someone else with him, but Drew couldn't get a good look at the second man. Sykes? If Drew had been alone, he would have gone back for Sykes. Was it him?

Blue raised a rifle to his shoulder and took aim. Their bobbing heads in the water were a small target, but a decent hunting rifle was accurate up to three hundred yards.

"Take a breath, Melinda. We're going under."

"What?"

"Underwater. Now."

He waited until he saw her inhale. Then he coiled his arm around her waist and dove down. Below the surface, he felt the subtle pull of a current moving in the direction he wanted to go, away from shore. Diffused sunlight glowed on the water above them. Below was murky darkness and the specter of drowning.

He dragged her back to the surface. They both gasped.

When he looked back at the shore, Blue had lowered his rifle.

"Not doing that again," Melinda said.

"Okay."

"I mean it."

"Okay. Keep swimming."

Blue still hadn't lifted his rifle. Drew was fairly certain that he wasn't supposed to kill them. His assignment would be to capture them, especially

Melinda. Sykes wanted her alive. He wanted the baby that was growing inside her.

They neared the center of the lake where the finger of land reached toward them. Once they were on the other side, they'd be out of sight. Out of range.

Melinda's clean strokes had become a desperate flailing, but she kept kicking, kept making forward progress.

"Just a little farther," he encouraged her.

They rounded the spit of land.

That was when he heard the rush of a waterfall.

AT THE SPIT OF LAND, Melinda lowered her feet to the lake bottom and stood, up to her hips in water. She'd never been so cold, and that was saying a lot. She was a Minnesota girl.

Dragged down by her sodden clothing, she slogged through the water and headed toward dry land.

"Wait," Drew said.

"I'm freezing to death."

"Not really. Your body won't go into hypothermia."

He'd also told her that she would have incredible stamina, but her legs and arms ached. Her skin prickled. Shivers raced through her.

He strode up beside her. "This isn't the best

place for us to get out of the water. Sure, we've put some distance between us and Blue. But if he's got an all-terrain vehicle, he'll catch up fast."

A large flat rock on the land beckoned to her. It looked as comfortable as an overstuffed sofa. All she wanted was to stretch out there and lie in the sun. "Do you have a plan?"

He pointed, and her gaze followed the direction of his finger. She heard the churning and realized that a current pulled at her legs. "A waterfall? Please tell me you're not suggesting that we go over a waterfall."

He strode through the water toward the shore. In a little cove, there was a fallen log, worn smooth by being in the water. "We can use this."

"Do you have any idea how steep this waterfall is?"

"I'm hoping that it's a gradual descent into the rapids, not even as bad as the ones in Sioux Falls."

"But you don't know."

"Here's what I can tell you for certain," he said. "If Blue catches us, we'll never see the light of day again."

As she stood, dripping, she realized that her body was already beginning to recover. Though she felt the bite of the cold, it was more like the tingling when her foot fell asleep than a deep, unbearable pain.

She grumbled, "I can't believe I'm even considering your plan. You know I don't like to take risks."

He struggled in the shallow water to free the log from the surrounding branches. "Try to think of this as a white-water rafting trip. People pay good money for those trips."

"Because they have guides and inflatable vests. Oh, yes, and rafts."

"Yeah, yeah. Come over here and give me a hand."

She waded toward him. Trusting him was one thing. Hurling herself over a waterfall was quite another. But she didn't want to be caught. Blue would deliver her to Sykes, and that terrible man would not only hurt her, but he'd also experiment on her baby. *That couldn't happen.*

They wedged the log free. The weathered chunk of wood wasn't as big as she'd thought, probably only four feet in length. It bobbed in the water like a raft.

Drew shoved the log away from the shore. "Hang on before the current catches it."

She swam up beside him. Her arms clung to the chunk of wood. Her legs stretched out behind her. "You know this is crazy, don't you?"

"Hearing you say that makes me feel nostalgic. You haven't called me crazy in hours."

The expanse of lake that stretched before them was twice the length that they swam to reach the spit of land in the middle, but their forward progress was a hundred times easier because the current was stronger. If she hadn't been freezing cold and running for her life, she might have enjoyed the view of rugged hillsides, shimmering waters and blue sky.

"We can do this," Drew said. "We've got the advantage."

Not unless desperation counted as a plus. "How do you figure?"

"Blue is just a henchman. But you and me? We've got motivation. We've got everything to live for."

"And?" she asked.

"We'll make it."

With all her heart, she wanted to believe him. She clung to the hope that they'd come out of this all right. They needed luck, needed for Helga the troll to watch over them and keep them safe.

The rumble of the waterfall grew louder.

She paddled with her feet. Her sodden jeans rubbed together, chafing her legs. "When we get to the falls, what should I do?"

"Don't fight the current. Let it pull you along."

"Well, gosh, I should be good at that. Ever since I met you, that's what I've been doing. Letting you pull me along."

"I haven't steered you wrong."

"Say that again on the other side of the water-fall."

He turned her face toward him and gave her a quick kiss. His face was pale, and his wet hair stuck to his forehead. Even so, he was the most handsome man she'd ever seen.

When she faced forward, she glimpsed the churning white water. Anticipation rose within her—anticipation and dread and the beginning of screaming panic. There was nothing she could do but hang on and pray.

The closer they got to the falls, the faster they were pulled through the water. Drew had told her that he liked to go fast; he was probably enjoying this ride.

"When we go over the ledge," he yelled over the noise, "hold your breath."

Second thoughts nearly overwhelmed her, but there was no way to turn back now. The force of the water was too strong to fight. Whether she liked it or not, she was committed.

The rushing water whipped them over the edge. Clinging to the log, she was propelled forward. The drop was four or five feet, but it felt like a mile. Roiling water crashed over her head. She submerged. Didn't know if she was upside down or right side up. Her hip banged against a rock.

Then she was breathing again, still hanging on to the log.

They'd made it over the falls. Drew was still beside her. And the white water continued to pull them downstream.

"Are you okay?" he yelled.

"I think so."

They soared through the water, swept along at an amazing speed. The log bashed against rocks. They entered a canyon with a rock wall on one side. Swooping, they raced over another smaller waterfall.

Her squeal of panic turned into laughter. Excitement rushed through her. This was fun. Still, she didn't want to push their luck. "We should get out."

"Not yet. The water is moving faster than we could walk."

The creek narrowed, and they encountered more white water. More speed. Still fun. But her fingers were numb; she was losing her grip on the log. "I can't hold on."

He repositioned himself so his arm held her against the log. Under the white water, her leg whacked against another rock. She felt the pain but knew there would be no bruise. She was invincible. They both were.

The creek stretched into a wider space and the

water calmed enough for Drew to pull her toward land. Her knees dragged against the bottom.

As she released her grip on the log, Drew supported her weight and lifted her to her feet. Together, they staggered from the water.

Though she hadn't planned to kiss dry land, her legs gave out, and she dropped to her hands and knees. From there, she sprawled face-first onto the rocky earth. She'd survived. Unbelievable. And her Swiss Army watch was still ticking.

She rolled to her back and stared up at the sky. The sun had climbed higher. She closed her eyes, and allowed the warm rays to beam over her.

Drew sat beside her, casting a shadow. "How are you doing?"

Good question. She hadn't sustained any serious injuries. "It feels like I'm still in the water. Rushing along. We were going pretty fast."

"We were," he agreed.

Blinking, she looked up at him. "I liked it. The speedy part. Not that I'm planning to make this a hobby. But rocketing over the waterfall and down the creek was kind of, um, exhilarating."

"I'm glad." He raked his wet hair off his forehead. "If our child takes after me, you're in for a lifetime of thrills."

There were worse fates than being the mother of a hereditary daredevil. "First, I'd like to take a nap."

"I know you're tired," he said. "Your body is working at healing itself. But we need to keep moving."

"I know. Claudia said we should find a road where they can pick us up."

With a groan, she sat up. He caught hold of her hand and brought her to her feet. Squinting against the sun, she looked back at the white water. Far in the distance, she saw the waterfall. "It doesn't look anywhere near as treacherous as it felt when we crashed over it."

"Those were some serious rapids," he said. "I'd call it class four, maybe even class five."

"What does that mean?"

"Ratings given for rafters and kayakers. This stretch of white water was expert level."

"Wow, I'm an expert. That should look good on my resume."

He wrapped his arms around her, molding her to his chest. Their wet clothing stuck together. She was grateful for his strong arms holding her up.

"Melinda, can you forgive me?"

"For what?"

"I'm supposed to be protecting you. Instead, I put you directly in the line of fire."

"It was my choice to come along."

"I should have known better," he said.

Though it was imprudent and irrational, she

really was glad to be here with him. This escape could have turned out badly, but that didn't happen. She had an experience that she'd never forget—something to tell the grandchildren. Their grandchildren. "Actually, I want to thank you."

"Okay." His voice sounded a wary note. "I'm not exactly sure why."

"All my life, I've been a good girl." A librarian, for goodness' sake. Nobody would ever call her a risk-taker. "I've been reliable and sensible and safe. But not anymore."

With his thumb, he tilted her chin so that she looked up into his eyes. "Who are you now?"

"A wild, exotic woman. Fearless in the face of danger. I've turned into the kind of woman I used to read about. And I like it, Drew. I like the new me."

"So do I."

His kiss warmed her and gave her strength to face the next challenge. Or the next disaster.

Chapter Seventeen

Finding an accessible place to wait for Jack and Claudia to pick them up wasn't too hard. After about fifteen minutes of hiking, Drew spotted a gravel two-lane road that wound through the forests, following the twists and curves of Spiney-Piney Creek. He wasn't surprised. People tended to settle near water, which meant they needed access. He assumed there were cabins in this area.

Though Melinda put up a good front, he knew she was exhausted and headachy. After years of experience, he had less trouble adapting to the aftermath of self-healing. Sure, he wanted to sleep and to quell the hammering inside his skull. But he could keep going.

At the edge of the road, she balked. "If this is the only road in the area, Blue will find it."

"You catch on fast."

When she looked up at him, her eyelids drooped with the effort of staying awake. "What do we do?"

"Hide."

He found them a nest on a cliff overlooking the road. They were hidden from view by a craggy rock and a couple of trees. He snuggled Melinda against his chest. Within minutes, she was sound asleep.

Though he kept watch, he relaxed his muscles and emptied his mind, putting himself into a meditative state that mimicked sleep and facilitated his recovery to full strength.

He came alert only once when a truck drove along the road. From his vantage point, Drew glimpsed the driver. A young man with a thick black beard.

Not Blue. Not Sykes. Was it the other person he'd seen on the shore? He couldn't exert the mental energy to think about that now. But he needed to know what they were facing.

Even with the implanted GPS chip, it took Jack and Claudia over an hour to locate them. Their SUV stopped just below their hiding place on the cliff. Both Jack and Claudia emerged from the car and looked around.

Drew roused himself and waved. Melinda was still zonked out, and he carried her down the sloping hill.

"Is she all right?" Claudia asked.

"She needs sleep." As he tucked her into the

back of the SUV, he explained, "In the self-healing process, blood rushes to the injury, depriving the brain. The result is exhaustion and a headache."

Claudia still looked concerned. "Melinda was injured?"

"We went over a waterfall and got banged around on the rocks pretty good."

She gaped.

"Over a waterfall?" Jack gave a short laugh. "You've got an amazing ability. Want to trade?"

"I wouldn't mind." He climbed in beside Melinda and arranged her on the seat with her head on his lap. "I'd like to have more brain power, at least enough to remember what happened to me when I was a kid. That's why we went to The Facility. I was hoping to spark some kind of memory."

"Did it work?" Claudia asked as she gave him a couple of blankets.

"Not much." Drew covered Melinda with one of the blankets. Their clothes were still damp, and he placed the second blanket on his thigh to make her a pillow. She snuggled until she got comfortable. Though still asleep, a smile curved her lips.

Gently, he stroked her shoulder. Never again would he put her in danger. Never.

Jack got behind the steering wheel. "Where to?"

Drew noted the time on the dashboard clock. It was already after noon. Too late for his rendezvous with Harlan? His foster father had promised to wait for him, but Drew wanted to take some time to rethink their plans. His impulsive dash to The Facility had almost cost them their lives.

Though he hated to share the location of his cabin, he trusted Jack and Claudia. "We're going home."

He gave them the nearest crossroads for the cabin, which Claudia plugged into her self-contained GPS system. Then she turned around in her seat to face Drew. "Tell us what happened when you went to The Facility."

As he related the events, he realized that his headache was mostly gone. His body had healed itself, and he could only hope that Melinda's body had responded in the same way, which meant the baby was unharmed.

Drew ended his narrative with what, in his view, was the most important piece of information. "Someone was with Blue."

"Sykes?" Jack suggested.

"Could be. When I looked at the DVD, I remembered seeing Sykes while I was being pursued in Europe. He and Blue could be a team."

"Or he could still be in Europe," Jack said. "Some of the people who are financing him are international."

"But Harlan says he's here in the States," Claudia said. "Should I call him, Drew? Tell him that you won't be able to make the meeting?"

"Make the call," Drew said. "I'll talk to him."

Though he still didn't trust his foster father, Harlan was their best connection to Sykes. He took the cell phone from Claudia.

When Harlan answered, Drew was terse. "I can't make it."

"Are you all right, son?"

Son? Why did he continue to make that connection? The whole time Drew lived with him, Harlan was a marginal father at best. "I'm fine. Melinda's fine. And I'm not interested in playing any more games. Can you set up the meet with Sykes?"

"The only way that's going to work is if I can convince him that you've decided to quit running and turn yourself in. We both have to talk to him on the phone. Together."

"Not necessary," Drew said. "We can patch together a connection."

"Sykes has top-of-the-line technology. He'll know if we try to pull a fast one."

"Is he in the area?" Drew asked. "I'm not turning myself in to one of his henchmen."

"I don't know for sure where Sykes is," Harlan admitted. "When I contact him, he'll give me the information. As long as I have you with me."

"I'll meet you at the house in Lead, tomorrow."

"Sooner is better." He chuckled. "You always were a procrastinator. Never did your homework until the last minute. I remember—"

"Make it tonight." Drew didn't want to walk down memory lane. "Seven o'clock."

He ended the call and held the phone out to Claudia. "You'd better turn this off. I don't want Harlan to be able to track our location."

"This is a satellite phone," she said. "It can't be traced, but I'll turn it off anyway."

"I'll meet him tonight at seven. In Lead."

While they discussed pros and cons, Drew decided that he was inclined to go through with the meeting as long as Melinda wasn't involved. He wanted to keep her as far away from Sykes as possible, and he still didn't trust Harlan.

In the back of his mind, he considered taking Melinda and going on the run. He looked down at her as she slept, and a gentle warmth spread through him. Her safety was the most important thing—the only thing.

A question from Claudia interrupted his thoughts. "When you went to The Facility, did you have any memories?"

"I started to have glimmers, but we really didn't get inside the cave."

"I have some other photos," she said.

He shrugged. "I'll take a look."

"These are disturbing pictures," she warned. "There were people who died at The Facility and were kept in a cold storage morgue. Do you still want to see them?"

"I can take it."

She handed over a folder. "Most of these people have been identified using DNA samples. If you recognize them or have further information regarding their connection to the experiments, it would be useful."

He looked at the cold, dead face of a young boy who couldn't have been more than eight. Only a child. "My God, how could this happen?"

"That boy was abducted when he was five."

Drew forced himself to confront the photo. "I don't recognize the boy."

Drew looked at another picture. A teenaged boy. In life, he might have been handsome. In death, his cheeks were sunken. His skin was ashen.

"We don't have an ID for this young man," Claudia said. "Any information you can give us would help."

Drew shook his head. "I've got nothing."

"The next one is a woman. She was in the first trimester of pregnancy, and the fetus was removed postmortem. Her name is—"

"Pamela," Drew said. "Pamela Forbes."

He stared down at the picture of his New York girlfriend, the woman he'd proposed to. He'd bought her an engagement ring and told her he loved her.

Pamela was dead. The fetus—his child—was dead.

His heart stopped beating.

All thoughts of running were erased from his mind. Drew would do whatever it took to bring Sykes down.

AT THE CABIN, Melinda felt rested. As she changed into dry clothes in the bathroom, she inspected her legs and arms for injuries and found nary a bruise. The ability to self-heal made no sense whatsoever, but she was grateful for this gift. Without it, she'd have been battered and beaten and probably hypothermic.

She slipped into a fresh pair of jeans and checked out her reflection in the mirror over the sink. Yikes! A matted mass of tangles sprang from her head. Too bad self-healing didn't extend to making her hair look good.

Dragging her brush through the snarls, she belatedly recalled that she hadn't gotten conditioner when they picked up the other groceries.

It was a relatively unimportant lapse of memory, unlike much of what had been going on.

When she'd awakened in the car, she'd been surprised that Drew was willing to share the location of his secret hideout. Something about him had changed. He was dark. Brooding. Angry.

When the bathroom door opened and he came inside, she dropped her brush and went to him. His jaw was rigid. His eyes burned with a dangerous fire. "What is it?" she asked.

"Pamela."

It took a moment for her to make the connection. "Your girlfriend in New York? The one who left you?"

"She's dead." He breathed hard. His nostrils flared. "They found her body in the morgue at The Facility."

She remembered that Pamela had been pregnant. "And the baby?"

"Pamela was in the first trimester." His voice choked. "The fetus wasn't viable. They're dead. Both dead."

When she reached toward him to comfort him, he held up his hand, keeping her at a distance. She knew that he wasn't accustomed to having anyone share his pain, but she was here for him. She cared so deeply about him. "Let me hold you."

"It's my fault. My goddamn fault. If it hadn't been for me—" His rage erupted. He pivoted and leaned both hands against the wall. With a guttural curse, he slammed his fist through the wallboard.

There was nothing she could do or say to make him feel better, but she had to try. Reaching out, she rested her hand on his back. Gradually, she eased her hand around until her arm encircled him. She pressed her cheek against his back. He was so tense that he trembled.

Abruptly, he turned, pulled her against his chest and held her tightly. They stood that way for several minutes, clinging to each other, trying to make sense of an unthinkable horror.

His voice was a taut whisper. "When I proposed to her, she told me that she was going to have an abortion, that she was leaving me for someone else, that she'd gotten a well-paying job in Paris. If I'd been paying attention to what she said instead of feeling sorry for myself, I would have known she was lying. Pamela wasn't a high-powered businesswoman."

"Sykes must have gotten to her," Melinda said. "He's a powerful man. He could have promised her the moon."

"I should have known."

But he couldn't have known that Sykes was close. At that time, Drew didn't know about The

Facility. He was in hiding. "If Sykes knew about Pamela, he must have known where you were."

"Why didn't he take me?"

Because he wanted the baby. She felt the danger coming closer, wrapping around her like a web made of steel. Finding out about Pamela had to be devastating for Drew, but she couldn't allow him to sink into despair. "We have to fight. We have to end this."

"I can't think." His grip on her loosened. "My head is exploding."

He needed the time to mourn. But not right now. They needed to be smart. She patted his chest. The fabric of his shirt was still damp. "It's hard to believe that Sykes would let you go. If he knew where you were, why didn't he scoop you up into his net?"

When he shrugged, he leaned back against the bathroom wall. His arms dropped to his sides. "I don't know."

"There's something that's been bothering me. Blue was waiting for us at The Facility. It's almost like he knew we were going to be there."

"That's impossible," he said. "We didn't tell anybody."

She nodded. "It's like when we crossed the Missouri at Pierre and were followed. How could anyone guess that we'd choose that particular place to cross?"

"Not why," he said. "The question is—who?"

"Do you know?" she asked.

"When I was a kid, I went to Pierre with Harlan. I have good memories of the place. He could have had a hunch that I'd cross there."

She agreed. "And Harlan knows you well enough to realize that as soon as you knew the location of The Facility, you'd go there."

"I saw somebody else with Blue at the lake."

"Harlan," she said. "And I know a way to prove it was him."

Chapter Eighteen

Melinda emerged from the bathroom, went directly to the desk with the computer and started rummaging through her purse. Thank goodness she hadn't taken it on the Harley! She found her little red cell phone, held it up and announced, "I've figured out a major clue."

From the kitchen area, Jack and Claudia watched her warily. They'd probably heard Drew punching through the wall. His violent behavior shouldn't be condoned, but Melinda understood why he needed to vent, and she had no intention of getting into an anger management discussion.

She waved to Claudia. "I'm going to need your help."

"Sure thing." Claudia came toward her. "What's up?"

"Back in Sioux Falls," Melinda said, "when we were trying to get out of town, Blue was on our trail. But there was someone else working with him. A mystery man."

Jack looked toward Drew. "And you said there was another man at the lake."

"Correct," Drew said. "A shadow figure who creeps around the edges, just out of reach. He's plagued me for years. If Melinda is right, that mystery man is Harlan."

"Can't be." Claudia shook her head. "He's FBI. I've checked his credentials."

"I can identify him," Melinda said, gesturing with her cell phone. "I have a witness who was approached by the man working with Blue."

Drew gave her a grin. "Lily the librarian."

She was glad to see his tension beginning to abate. If they worked together, they could do anything. She explained to Jack and Claudia, "Before we left Sioux Falls, I was supposed to stop at the library where I work. Drew convinced me otherwise, which turned out to be a very smart move because there was a stranger in the library asking about me."

"Which doesn't necessarily mean he was working with Blue," Claudia said.

"We can find out." Melinda was proud of herself for making these deductions. Those mystery book detectives had nothing on her. "Lily Rhoades, my supervisor, took notice of this person. She thought he was an attractive, older man. Can we e-mail Harlan's photo to Lily?"

"No problem." Claudia sat in the chair behind the computer. "I'll pull his FBI ID photo off another site."

While Claudia worked her magic with the computer, Melinda hit the speed-dial number on her phone that would ring through to the head librarian's desk.

"Augustana Library. Lily speaking."

"It's Melinda. I need your help."

"Are you feeling better?"

It took a second for Melinda to recall that she was supposed to be taking a couple of days off on sick leave. The break-in at her apartment seemed like a lifetime ago. "Much better, thank you."

"Who wouldn't be? You're with that hot reporter guy, right?"

She glanced at Drew. Though his still-damp clothes were disheveled and he was wracked by intense emotion, he was most definitely hot. "Right."

"He'd better be taking real good care of you. Or else he'll have to answer to me."

After all Drew had been through, Melinda doubted that he'd be intimidated by a feisty librarian. "Do you remember the man who came into the library looking for me?"

"Sure enough," Lily said. "Nice-looking fellow. Just the right age for an old bird like me."

"I'm going to send you an e-mail photo on the front desk computer, and you tell me if it's the same guy."

"Okeydokey."

Melinda consulted with Claudia, giving her the e-mail address for the library computer. The ID photo for Harlan showed a pleasant-looking man in his mid-fifties with graying hair. He was a bit thick in the jowls, and his nose seemed too small for the rest of his face. Otherwise, he was remarkably average.

"It's sent," Claudia said.

Melinda held the cell phone to her mouth. "Lily? Did you get the picture?"

"Hold your horses, kiddo. I'm checking ri-i-i-ight now." There was a pause, then she said, "That's him, all right. But he's better-looking in person. Has a twinkle in his eye. Is he single?"

"Trust me," Melinda said, "you wouldn't like this guy."

She gave Drew a thumbs-up signal. Now, they had proof. An eyewitness had placed Harlan in Sioux Falls. He'd been sneaking around, trying to locate her, which meant he was probably working with Blue.

After she promised Lily a full report with all the

details as soon as she was back in town, Melinda disconnected the call and turned off her phone.

Drew paced, and Jack stood with arms crossed. The lack of furniture in the small cabin made their conversation seem like a confrontation. The only way they could get comfortable would be to sit on the mattress, and she doubted these two men would go along with that suggestion.

"He's working for Sykes," Drew said. "Harlan admitted to me that when he was my foster father, Sykes paid him to keep an eye on me. Taking payoffs is sure as hell not standard procedure for the FBI."

"I'm not defending him," Jack said. "I don't even know the guy. We've never met."

Drew continued to pace as he talked. "Here's what I think. Harlan figured out that I'd gone to New York."

She intercepted him. "Your pacing is making me dizzy. Let's go outside."

"Fine." He flipped the locks on the door. "When I was in hiding in New York, I thought I was tricky. I changed my name a half dozen times. Every time I sensed someone getting too close, I moved. But there was one thing I couldn't change."

Melinda nodded. "Your writing."

"I was doing articles for sports magazines—

Harlan's favorite reading material. He must have noticed something in the phrasing. And he tracked me down."

When Drew flung open the door, all four of them spilled outside, leaving the confines of the cabin. Melinda inhaled a breath of clean mountain air, and the others did the same. The level of intensity dropped to a more bearable level.

Jack cleared his throat. "Okay, Drew. If your reasoning is correct and Harlan managed to figure out who you were and where you were, why didn't he take you back to Sykes?"

"That's easy," Claudia piped up. "Sykes was paying him to search. It was more profitable for Harlan to let Drew run free."

Drew looked to the treetops as though seeking answers in the sky. "He told me that he protected me. In a way, I guess he did. If it wasn't for Harlan, I would have been locked up in a cage. Instead, Pamela took my place."

A silence fell as the mountain wind swirled around them. Melinda knew they were all thinking about Pamela's death. And the unfortunate fates of the other victims. Abducted children. Young men and women used for experiments. Though The Facility had been dismantled, those experiments could be continuing.

It had to be stopped. Sykes had to be stopped.

Melinda straightened her shoulders. "What can we do?"

"Let's go back to the original plan," Drew said. "We set a trap for Harlan. And I'll be the bait."

Melinda threw her hands in the air. "That's just about the worst idea I've ever heard."

"Have you got a better plan?"

She didn't.

THERE WASN'T MUCH TIME for planning. Drew had agreed to meet Harlan in Lead at seven o'clock, and it was three forty-five right now. He and Jack should go to the house right away, before dark, so they could set up an ambush for Harlan and Blue.

Jack was on the satellite phone with the FBI agent he trusted. From what Drew heard of the conversation, Jack was careful about telling enough but not too much.

Claudia had gone to work on the computer, trying to track down solid evidence from Harlan's bank accounts and credit lines. If he'd been taking payoffs from Sykes all these years, there had to be a paper trail.

What could he have done with the money? During the time Drew had lived with Harlan and Belle, he never noticed extravagant spending. They'd lived a simple life with no special vacations or lavish purchases. The opposite, in fact.

Belle had clipped coupons and saved up to buy a new vacuum cleaner.

In the storage room next to the bathroom, he sorted through his stockpile of weaponry, trying to decide how he could incapacitate Blue. Shooting him was one option. But Blue might be a valuable source of information. The better course would be to use a flash-bang explosive that would momentarily blind and deafen the big man without causing permanent physical damage.

Melinda stepped into the room, closed the door and leaned against it. She raised her voice so he could hear her over the steady hum of the generator. "Don't go."

"There's no choice. I can't let Harlan get away with this."

"I'm not saying you should let him off the hook. But why not let Jack's friend at the FBI deal with his capture?"

"Because the Feds have to play by the rules," he said. "I don't."

"What does that mean?" She stalked toward him. "You're not going to kill him, are you?"

Though Drew had a hell of a lot of good reasons to hate his foster dad, he wasn't planning a murder. "I need to keep him alive. Harlan is our link with Sykes."

"Sykes." Her lips curled in disgust as she spoke

his name. "What makes you think Harlan will give him to you?"

For a bastard like Harlan, motivations were simple: money and survival. Drew couldn't offer the big bucks Sykes would be paying, but he could give Harlan something that the FBI couldn't. "I'll offer him a deal. If he gives me Sykes, I won't take him into custody."

"What?"

"Here's how it works," he said. "If Harlan is arrested by the Feds, they'll send him directly to prison. Once the FBI learns about his double cross, he'll be branded a traitor. That's not a charge they'll be likely to forgive."

"You'd let him go free?"

"Not exactly. He'll be on the run." Drew liked the symmetry. For the past ten years, he'd been looking over his shoulder. Now, Harlan would be living that dark existence, afraid to come out from the shadows. "The FBI will be in pursuit."

"What about Blue?"

Drew surveyed his weapons. "I can deal with him."

"It's too risky." As she came closer, he saw the concern in her eyes. "You think you're inde-structible, but you've never been shot."

"Thanks for reminding me."

"Please, Drew. I can't stand to lose you."

He reached out and laid his hand on the side of her face. Her cheeks were hot and flushed. Her lips pressed together. When he brushed the line of her mouth with his thumb, he thought she might bite him. "Don't worry, Melinda. I always survive."

"You don't know that." She tore his hand away from her face. "This isn't like one of your extreme-sporting events."

In a way, it was. He felt the same anticipation, the rush of adrenaline through his veins. His self-healing ability had taught him to be fearless. "I'll make it."

Her eyes squeezed shut as though she was holding back tears. "What if you're wrong?"

"Don't cry, Melinda."

He folded her into his arms. Never before in his life had anyone cared enough to be worried about his survival, and he understood why she was scared. She didn't take risks. Even though she claimed to be a different person after they went over the waterfall, she was still a librarian at heart.

Her voice trembled. "You said it yourself, Drew. We have everything to live for."

"What kind of future would we have if we're on the run? I don't want that life for my child."

"The FBI would offer us protective custody."

"Another cage." Years ago, he could have turned

himself in to the authorities. He knew the value of his self-healing ability, and he didn't want to be a subject of experiments. Not for Sykes or anybody else. "I can't do that."

She tilted her head back and looked up at him. Tears streaked her cheeks. "Then take me with you."

"You're staying here with Claudia." He caressed her shoulders. "You've got to trust me. I'm doing the right thing."

"Is there any way I can change your mind?"

This was about more than changing his mind. *She wanted to change him*. To tame his risk-taking behavior. To have him settle down with her for a quiet life of child-rearing. Could he handle that kind of existence? Probably not. He'd never been normal.

He kissed her forehead. If she was right and he didn't make it through this confrontation in one piece, he wanted to be sure she'd be all right. "Come over here. I have something to show you."

He led her to a three-foot-square, fireproof combination safe in the corner of the room. Inside were most of the important documents in his life. Checking account information, the deed for the cabin, the ownership documents for the Range Rover, the SUV he'd left behind in Pierre and the motorcycle that he'd probably never see again.

And cash. He wasn't sure how much but it was a significant amount—enough to get her started on a life of her own after the baby was born.

She eyed the safe suspiciously. "What's in there?"

He squatted down to the level of the combination lock. "Paperwork. A deed. Pink slips for my vehicles. Some cash."

"Why would you leave such important information here in the wilderness? Weren't you worried about a break-in?"

"Number one," he said, "I left it here because I don't trust banks or lawyers. Number two, I've taken security precautions. Watch me carefully."

"You and your security." She tsk-tsked as she leaned over his shoulder. "The word *paranoid* is popping to mind again."

He flipped the combination lock in the most obvious combination: one-two-three. It clicked. "Here's the good part," he said. "If you twist the handle on the safe now, it doesn't open. It fires off an explosive charge. Likewise, if you try to lift the safe and carry it, ka-boom. To disarm the device, dial the combination lock back to zero. Then it opens without problem."

Her eyes were wide. "You rigged a bomb?"

"It's not a big charge. Nothing that would destroy the cabin or start a forest fire. Somebody standing ten feet back probably wouldn't be hurt. The explosion is just enough to convince who- ever's messing with my stuff to back off."

She paced away from him, then returned to his side. "Why are you showing me this?"

"I've been listening to what you've been saying. And I agree that there's a chance—a minuscule outside chance—that I won't make it. If the worst happens, I want you and the baby to be cared for."

"Even if there's a million dollars in that safe, it's not enough. I don't want your stuff. I want you."

He stood to face her. "I can't change who I am."

"A risk-taker," she said bitterly. "This is differ- ent. I'm not trying to hold you back."

"Yeah, you are."

"You could be killed, and I don't want to be telling our child bedtime stories about what his father was like before he died. I want our child to know you, to see your smile, to hear your voice. I want you to be a real father. Not a memory."

And he wanted the same thing. Drew knew what it was like to grow up without parents, and his child deserved better. But he couldn't back down and hope that law enforcement would catch Sykes. He had to go after Harlan. "We're leaving now to prepare for the meet at seven. It's all going to be all right. We'll return by eight."

She stripped off her Swiss Army watch and handed it to him. "Your watch is broken. You might need this."

"It was a gift." When he first gave her the watch, he'd planned to leave her. The watch was supposed to be something for her to remember him by. "Don't you want it?"

"Bring it back to me. At eight o'clock."

He slipped the watch in his pocket. If he didn't survive this meeting, it would be best if she forgot all about him.

Chapter Nineteen

On the drive to Lead, Drew tried not to think about Melinda. Her anger bugged him, but he could handle hostility and rejection. No big deal. He was a lone wolf, didn't need anybody else. But he couldn't forget her tears. She cared enough about him that she'd wept.

And how did he respond to her? To the mother of his child? He turned his back and went ahead with his plan.

It had to be this way. He had to find Sykes.

Setting his jaw, he focused one hundred percent on setting their trap for Harlan. Though he recalled every inch of the house where he'd grown up, he'd left ten years ago. The place would be different now. Apparently, no one was living there. Harlan never would have chosen that location for their meeting if someone else had been in the house. Other families must have come and gone.

In the passenger seat of the Range Rover, Jack stared through the windshield with alert curiosity as though memorizing the rugged mountain terrain. He remarked, "Claudia still hasn't found proof that Harlan was taking money from Sykes."

"He admitted to it."

"I'd feel a lot better about confronting him if we had more evidence to lay in front of him."

"We have a witness," Drew reminded him.

"But Harlan can come up with another excuses for why he talked to the librarian. If we're going to use the threat of FBI charges to make him cooperate, we need something that'll stick."

"He told me that he got cash from Sykes when I was living at his house. He—" Drew hesitated, recalling that Harlan had said something more.

Jack looked toward him. "What else?"

"He said it wasn't about the money. But what else could have motivated him to work for Sykes? Harlan isn't a scientist, so he wouldn't have cared about the research per se."

"He could have a grudge against the FBI."

"I don't think so. He's not a man ruled by his passions. He's Joe Average. The kind of guy who likes to have a beer and watch sports on the tube." What would cause an average guy to betray his work and participate in the heinous crimes perpetrated at The Facility? "It's got to be money."

Driving through the small town of Lead, Drew clicked through memories. The drugstore on the corner. The Elks Lodge. The gas station. A couple of storefronts on the main drag were vacant, but the town seemed to be doing okay. A good number of cars and trucks parked at the curb outside the café.

Lead was smaller than he remembered, as though he was looking back through the wrong end of a telescope. He took a left at the square brick grade school, where a couple of kids were shooting hoops on the asphalt playground. "The house is only a couple more miles."

Jack startled as if waking up from a dream. "At the house, we need to look around. I see you making an important discovery. Something that's going to nail Harlan."

"Is this a pre-cog vision?"

"You could call it that. I see us going down the stairs into the basement."

"This object that we find," Drew said. "Do you know what it is?"

Jack shook his head. "Sorry."

Drew drove past the house without stopping. The exterior of the ranch-style house had been painted a cheerful yellow, but otherwise the surroundings hadn't changed too much. At this time of year, there were no flowers or leafy shrubs in the yard. He continued into the forest. The house

Drew grew up in—the Andersons' house—was secluded, separated from the other residences in the neighborhood by an acre of land on one side and wild forest on the other.

He turned down a small, winding road that doubled back in the direction they'd come. At the end of the road, he turned the vehicle around for a quick escape and parked. "We'll leave the car here so Harlan won't see it when he arrives."

Jack drew his automatic. Drew did the same. Not knowing what they might find in the house, they needed to proceed with caution. From the back of the Range Rover, they each grabbed a duffel bag filled with weapons.

Moving easily through the forest, Drew found a winding path that he'd walked a thousand times when he was a kid. At the edge of the trees, he signaled Jack to stop.

Dusk had already begun to settle. Long shadows from the pine trees reached into the backyard. He watched the windows and saw no lights from inside. No sign of movement.

When he set down his duffel bag, Jack did the same. Until they were sure there were no surprises inside the house, they needed to be able to move fast, unencumbered by their weaponry and equipment.

As they approached the back door, his heart beat faster. How many times had he walked through this door? How many times had Belle yelled at him not to let it slam? She never allowed him to come through the front and track up the carpet.

Standing on the concrete stoop, he reached for the doorknob. Locked, of course. Drew automatically looked to the left. Beside a rose bush, he spotted a fake rock. When he picked it up, he found the door key hidden inside. After all these years?

He unlocked the door and stepped into the kitchen. To the right was a beige counter, oak cabinets and appliances. To the left, a round table with four chairs. On a lazy Susan in the center of the table were cut-glass salt-and-pepper shakers, half-full. Plaid half curtains and a matching valance covered the window. The kitchen matched his memories—exactly matched.

This place was a time capsule. From the rose-colored trivet on the counter to the burn mark on the linoleum in front of the oven, nothing had changed. On the counter were the three glass figurines of bear cubs that Belle liked so much. Each wore a different collar in red, blue and green.

While Jack searched the rest of the house with his gun drawn, Drew stumbled through the arch into the front room. A layer of dust covered every horizontal surface, but the furniture was the same. And he remembered…

He had been lying on the flowered sofa. His eyelids had been half-closed. A sharp, driving pain radiated from his heart. His limbs were numb. A man with white hair hovered over him. Sykes. Harlan and Belle stood watching. Her eyes were hard and angry. Harlan said, "He's had enough."

Harlan had been there.

Drew shook off the memory. Harlan knew. He hadn't kept a distance from Sykes. He was a co-conspirator, as guilty as Sykes himself.

Jack came into the room with his gun in one hand and a cell phone in the other. "Nobody here. I'll tell Claudia."

Harlan kept this house. He hadn't sold it or rented it out. Why? Drew had to know.

Ignoring all the other rooms, he went to the basement door. Jack had a vision of him finding a clue down here. Like the upstairs, the finished basement was the same as it had been ten years ago. In the family room, the worn sofa still faced the boxy television set where he and Harlan had sat for hours watching football.

In the laundry room, he spotted two new sets of utility cabinets with wide double doors. These built-in closets were painted green to match the other walls in the room, and they went from floor to ceiling. A huge storage space. When he pulled at the handle, he noticed locks at the top and bottom of the cabinet door.

Jack stood behind him. "This is it. I saw you pulling on the handle."

"What comes next?"

"You tell me."

Though Drew could have been careful about picking the locks and opening the doors that stretched across fifteen feet of wall space, he didn't give a damn. The answers were here. Harlan might have stashed the money here.

Drew stepped back. With a steady hand, he shot off one lock, then the other. He opened the doors.

Inside was a pine coffin.

MELINDA RUBBED the place on her wrist where her Swiss Army watch had been. Her last words to Drew had been angry, and she regretted them. She wanted to be with him instead of stuck here in the cabin with the walls closing in on her.

Claudia sat in front of the computer, searching for evidence that could be used against Harlan.

Melinda asked, "When Jack called, are you sure he didn't mention anything about Drew?"

"All Jack said was that they made it to Lead and there was nobody in the house." She rose from the chair. "I know you're worried. So am I. But Jack isn't going to let anything bad happen. He's an incredibly gentle man, but he has the heart of a warrior. And Drew's no slouch."

"So many things could go wrong." She went to the door. "I can't stand being inside. I need to go for a run."

"Not a good idea. We're safe in here."

Melinda eyed the screens showing the views from Drew's surveillance cameras. And she knew there were motion sensors on the road that would set off an alarm if a car approached. The precautions made her feel even more claustrophobic. "Maybe just a walk? A chance to breathe fresh air?"

"We're a lot alike, you and me."

"I wish." She gave a self-deprecating grin. "You have it together. You're a hundred times cooler than I am."

"Before Jack came into my life, I was a Web designer, living a solitary existence. He's the most exciting thing that ever happened to me."

"Well, we have that in common. Drew is nothing like anyone I've ever known before."

"And you love him."

"Gosh." Melinda frowned. "We haven't talked about love. I'm pregnant with his baby. He's changed my life, but I don't know about love. Especially not after what I said to him before he left."

"Do you want to talk about it?"

She gazed longingly at the door. "I want to go outside."

"Okay." Claudia took a .22 automatic from the table and tucked it into her jacket pocket. "Let's walk."

Shyly, she asked, "Have you got a gun for me?"

"I think there's a rifle in the storage room, but the boys took all the other guns and stuff."

Because they didn't expect a threat to come in this direction. Nobody knew about this cabin. They should be safe for now.

IN THE LAUNDRY ROOM of the ranch-style house where he'd grown up, Drew opened the double doors to the second built-in cabinet and found a second coffin. What the hell had gone on in this house?

He turned toward Jack, who stood all the way across the room in the doorway with his arms folded across his chest.

"Melinda is always telling me I'm crazy," Drew said. "She has no idea. This is what crazy looks like."

"You said Harlan was Joe Average."

"I might have misjudged."

These long, deep cabinets hadn't been here when Drew was growing up; Harlan had constructed this basement burial place after Drew left. Kind of a macabre home improvement project. He imagined his foster father whistling as he gathered his toolbox from the workbench in the garage. Then, building the cabinets while having a beer and listening to the Brewers game on the radio. Why? What had he been thinking?

The lifetime of undercover work, constantly lying to Sykes and to the FBI, must have driven him over the edge into insanity. He'd hung on to this house, kept it exactly like it was and started collecting corpses in the basement.

The lids on both of these pine boxes were fastened with easy-to-open latches, but Drew hesitated. He didn't really want to see what was inside.

Jack took a step forward. "Should I?"

"I'll do it." In a way, finding coffins in the basement of his foster parents' home was fitting. His life as foster kid and the victim of genetic experimentation had always been one step away from madness.

He opened the lid on the first coffin. The body inside was shriveled to bone. Drew knew it was a woman because the skeleton was arranged inside a blue dress with a lace collar.

Jack looked over his shoulder. "Natural mummification?"

"That's an urban myth." When he lived in New York, he'd heard stories about people who had been dead in their apartments for years and naturally turned into mummies. "She might have been buried outside before being brought in here. Or soaked in lye. Something."

The right side of the skull showed considerable trauma, as though someone had held a gun to her head and pulled the trigger. Laid on top of her sunken chest was a locket.

Drew picked up the necklace. "This belonged to my foster mother, the woman I knew as Belle Anderson. Harlan told me they were divorced."

The silver locket was clean and shiny. Drew remembered how Belle used to hold it between her thumb and fingers, rubbing the filigreed pattern.

He opened the locket. Inside three ovals showed pictures of young boys. The children looked identical. Maybe it was only one boy wearing three different shirts in three different colors.

He dropped the locket into his jacket pocket and turned to the second coffin. He flipped the latch and opened the lid. The man inside had been embalmed; his skin was gray. He wore a suit with a red necktie. His head was shaved.

Jack made the identification. "This man was known as Red. I saw him kill himself about two months ago."

Even in death, he resembled Blue. "There were three of them, right? Red, Blue and Green."

"That's right."

The three little boys in the locket wore shirts of those colors. Drew recalled rumors that Harlan and Belle had lost their children. Three sons. If Sykes had taken Harlan's children for his experiments, it explained his hold on the FBI agent. To protect his kids, Harlan would have been forced to do as Sykes instructed.

"I think," Jack said, "that we have enough proof to make Harlan talk."

"Proof of insanity."

"Why do you think he wanted to meet you here? In this house?"

Some sort of revenge? Had he prepared another coffin for Drew? "I can't think of a single logical reason."

They closed the lids and shut the cabinet doors. Drew's natural instinct was to run. Fast.

Waiting for Harlan's arrival wasn't going to be easy. He didn't believe in ghosts, but the remains in the basement were a tangible presence.

As he entered the kitchen, he remembered Belle standing at the kitchen sink, looking out the window. Was she watching and waiting for her own three boys to come home? No wonder she'd never showed Drew any fondness. His presence was a reminder of what she'd lost.

He paced through the front room, trying to concentrate on how they could take Harlan into custody and eliminate the threat from Blue.

"We can't stay here," Jack said.

"Yeah, it's pretty creepy, but—"

"Seriously, we have to go. I'm sensing that Claudia is in danger."

"How do you—"

"I can feel it." His cell phone was already in his hand. "We need to get back to the cabin. Before it's too late."

Chapter Twenty

"Run!" Claudia snapped her cell phone closed.

Melinda responded to the urgency in her voice. She picked up her feet and moved. Back toward the cabin. They hadn't gone far, only about a hundred yards away from the front door.

Thin streaks of daylight resisted the murky gray dusk. It was difficult to see the rocks, twigs and pine cones on the path. In front of her, Claudia stumbled. She fell.

Melinda helped her to her feet. "That phone call. Was it Jack?"

"He said we were in danger. Told me to get in the car and drive away from the cabin. Get ourselves on the road to Lead."

Given his pre-cog abilities, Jack didn't need to give detailed explanations. He saw things before they happened. If he said there was danger, Melinda believed him. "Are you okay?"

"I twisted my ankle."

"Lean on me."

"I can make it." Claudia had taken the gun from her pocket. In her other hand, she held out the car keys. "You drive."

Together, they crossed the cleared area in front of the cabin.

Aware of the approaching danger, Melinda tried to be hypervigilent. She listened to rustling noises from the forest. She peered to the left, then to the right. Drew was good at scanning; his eyes were constantly in motion. But she saw nothing suspicious—only a shifting pattern of tree branches and shadows.

Near the car, the solid shape of a man appeared. How had he come so close? Claudia raised her arm to shoot, but he was faster. She was hit by a fiery bolt. A stun gun.

With a shout, Claudia went down.

Melinda squatted beside her. She took the gun, raised it and aimed in the direction where she'd seen the man. No one was there. He'd disappeared into the shadows.

She heard a sound from behind and whirled around.

Before she could squeeze off a shot, a second man kicked the weapon from her hand. She scrambled after it, but he picked up the .22.

"I'm not going to hurt you," he said. "You're too valuable, Melinda."

"Harlan." She recognized his voice from the phone call.

"I advise you to come along quietly."

She wanted to run. Her legs coiled like springs, prepared to leap. But she couldn't leave Claudia behind. *What should I do?* Her mind sifted through dozens of possibilities. She remembered Drew's warnings. If they fell into Sykes's hands, they'd never be seen or heard from again.

She had to stall. If she could get Harlan to take her into the cabin, she might figure out a way to rescue herself and Claudia.

Standing, she confronted Harlan. He was an average-looking man dressed all in black. His left hand, holding the .22, lowered to his side. In his right, he held an odd-looking gun. It could have been another stun gun. Or some kind of device to cause a blackout.

In either case, he hadn't zapped her. Which meant…what? He'd said he didn't want to hurt her.

"Why am I so valuable?" she asked.

"I think you know."

She glanced over her shoulder and saw the man who had fired his stun gun at Claudia. A black knit cap covered his shaved head, but there was no mistaking those huge shoulders. It was Blue.

Claudia moaned, and Melinda went down on her knees beside her fallen friend. "We have to help her."

"She'll be fine in a few minutes," Harlan said. "I assume her boyfriend is nearby. Where's Drew?"

There was no point in lying. "He's not here. He went to meet you in Lead."

"He went early to set a trap," Harlan said. "This time I outsmarted him."

"We should take the woman now." Blue's voice rumbled inside his barrel chest. "We'll come back for Drew."

Panic raced through her. If she allowed them to throw her in the back of a car, she'd never see daylight again. They'd carry her off to a new facility, another hellhole with cages. She couldn't let that happen, couldn't let them near her baby.

Her only chance was to play for time. Jack had called to warn them; he knew danger was close. Surely, he and Drew were on their way back here. If they arrived in time, Drew would make this right.

She clutched her belly, doubled over and groaned.

Harlan was beside her. "What's wrong with you?"

"It hurts. I need to lie down."

"Have you felt this pain before?" There was a note of real concern in his voice. "Is there bleeding?"

She groaned more loudly. "Please let me lie down."

Harlan wrapped his arm around her waist. "Know this, Melinda. If you try anything, your friend will be killed. Do you understand?"

She nodded and emitted a thin, frightened wail.

Harlan ordered Blue to carry Claudia inside as he escorted Melinda into the cabin. She knew there was a rifle in the storage room. And Drew's booby-trapped safe with the bomb. Maybe she could reach those weapons.

Blue placed Claudia on the floor near the kitchen. He slipped handcuffs onto her limp wrists. Taking a length of rope from his pocket, he tied her ankles.

As Melinda lowered herself onto the mattress, Harlan squatted beside her. "You'd better not be having a miscarriage. That's what happened with the other girl."

He was talking about Pamela, Drew's girlfriend from New York. "Did you…kidnap her?"

"She came along willingly after I promised a fancy job in Paris. I found her during one of the rare occasions when I managed to locate Drew. I thought I'd get both of them, but he disappeared." Over his shoulder, he called out an order. "Bring her some water."

"What happened to Pamela?" Claudia asked.

"There were problems with her pregnancy. She miscarried. They operated, but she didn't make it." He sounded irritated. "You're different than her. We've tested your blood. The fetus is thriving. I'm guessing that you've noticed some differences in yourself."

Trying to avoid giving him information he didn't already have, she changed the subject. "How did you find the cabin?"

"You slipped up," he said. "You used your little cell phone to call the Augustana Library, and I triangulated the signal."

Her clever, triumphant phone call to Lily had been their undoing. In her eagerness to prove Harlan was a bad guy, she'd betrayed their location. This was all her fault.

She groaned again. This time, for real.

WITH THE INTENSITY and focus of a Grand Prix driver, Drew careened along the winding mountain roads leading toward his cabin. In the passenger seat beside him, Jack tried to reach Claudia on the cell phone.

"No answer," Jack said.

Drew fishtailed around a hairpin curve. He saw two alternatives. The women had either been taken captive and were being driven to some unknown location or they were still at the cabin.

Though he hoped for the latter, he was scared as hell. Why wasn't Claudia answering the damn phone?

Though he hadn't spoken his question aloud, Jack answered. "The only reason she wouldn't answer is because she can't."

Somehow, Harlan had figured out where the cabin was. The son of a bitch was smart. Insane, but smart. "Harlan has them. They've been captured. Now what?"

"They could be on the road," Jack said. "We can track them using Melinda's GPS device."

Which might lead them directly to Sykes. Achieving that ultimate goal seemed unimportant compared to Melinda's safety. He never should have put her in danger. All she'd wanted was a peaceful, normal existence. He should have listened to her.

"If they're at the cabin," he said, "I know a way to get to the door without being picked up by my security cameras. It's a steep climb."

Jack braced his arm against the dashboard as the Range Rover whipped through another turn. "How much farther?"

"Fifteen minutes."

He was scared. More frightened than he'd ever been in his life. Those coffins in Lead convinced him that Harlan was insane, unpredictable. There was no telling what he'd do.

He shot a glance toward Jack. "Would it be too much to ask you for a vision?"

"I don't know how this is going to turn out."

Every person who was important to Drew had died. His parents. His high school girlfriend. Pamela.

He couldn't lose Melinda. She was gentle, resilient and strong. And he loved her. Why the hell hadn't he told her? Her survival and the survival of their child was all that mattered. He would rescue her or die trying.

MELINDA FEIGNED weakness. Though energy surged through her, she pretended that every gesture was a huge effort. She took a sip of water and collapsed back onto the mattress. Looking toward Harlan, she asked, "How much is Sykes paying you?"

"I don't care about the money."

He'd said that before, and she still didn't believe him. "Whatever the amount, I'll double it if you let us go."

"Nice try, Melinda." He shook his head and laughed. "You're a librarian. Not an heiress."

Blue came closer. "She might have a rich daddy."

"You saw her apartment," Harlan said. "That wasn't the home of a wealthy woman."

"It's Drew's money." She coughed and turned her

head away. She'd never been good at deception, and she didn't want Harlan to guess that she was laying a trap. "He has a safe. Right here at the cabin."

"And how did Drew get to be so rich?"

This part was the truth as she knew it. "He has an impressive job. You know that he flies all over the world. And you know that he's always in hiding. He doesn't trust banks. Keeps his money in cash."

Though Harlan scoffed, she could see that Blue was paying attention to her offer. He said, "I don't see a safe."

"Don't listen to her," Harlan snapped. "We have a plan. You know what we have to do."

"The plan." His heavy eyebrows pulled down in a scowl. Instead of looking angry, he appeared to be confused. "It wouldn't hurt to have some extra cash."

Melinda pointed toward the door to the storage room. "The safe is in there."

As Blue lumbered toward the door and turned on the light, Melinda glanced toward Claudia. Though she was awake enough to sit up, her eyes were still dazed. And her ankles were tied. Even if both Harlan and Blue went into the storage room and left them alone, they wouldn't be able to move quickly enough to make a run for it.

"She wasn't lying," Blue called out. "There's a safe."

"It could be a trap," Harlan warned. "Don't touch anything, son."

Son? Was Harlan using a term of endearment or was Blue really his offspring?

He rose slowly as though his joints ached. Though Harlan appeared to be in good shape, he wasn't a young man. The strain of double-crossing the FBI and dealing with Sykes had to be weighing heavily upon him.

At the front door of the cabin, he flipped the locks and turned on the overhead light. "I see Drew has arranged his usual precautions. Extra locks. Surveillance cameras. He's probably got some kind of emergency escape route from the cabin. Am I right?"

"Nothing I know of," Melinda said.

He paused at the computer display showing infrared displays of the surrounding forest. "He covered every approach to the cabin. If I closed these shutters, this place will be a self-contained fortress, ready for a siege."

She needed for him to keep the shutters open so Drew would know they were there. Trying to divert his attention, she said, "You could take the money in the safe and get away clean. There's no need to deal with Sykes."

Harlan pushed the door to the storage room wide open. "Get away from the safe, son. We're going."

"Not until we get this money."

"It's a combination lock. We don't have time to—"

Melinda volunteered, "I know how to open it."

Harlan shot an angry glare in her direction. "Why would you tell us?"

"To buy my freedom," she said. "You go your way. And we go ours. Nobody gets hurt."

Leaning his back against the wall, he studied her with suspicious eyes. "What's your angle? You can't be so naive that you think I'd let you go. There's nothing stopping me from taking Drew's money and getting a payoff from Sykes as well."

Except for Drew. If she could keep Harlan here long enough, Drew would arrive and figure out a way to stop him. "You were a federal agent for a long time. An honorable, law-abiding man. I want to believe that I can trust you."

"And if you can't?"

They both knew the answer to that question. If Harlan delivered her to Sykes, she'd lose everything.

Chapter Twenty-One

The lights shining from the cabin windows were clearly visible through the trees. From this downhill vantage point, Drew couldn't see inside. "What the hell is he doing?"

"Waiting for us," Jack said.

Harlan's goal must be to hand over all three of them—Melinda, Drew and Jack. A bonanza for Sykes.

Drew parked the Range Rover in such a way that the vehicle blocked the narrow road leading to the cabin. There would be no escape for Harlan and Blue in this direction.

Leaving the car, he told Jack, "There's a steep ledge that I didn't cover with surveillance cameras."

"Why not?"

"It's a tough climb, but we can make it. When we're at the top, it's only a couple of yards to the cabin."

"For those few yards, we'll be visible on camera."

"It's a chance we have to take."

"We can't bust through the door and start shooting," Jack said. "Not while Claudia and Melinda are hostages."

"You're right." Drew hadn't figured out what they'd do when they reached the cabin. Their advantage would be the element of surprise. The hard part would be figuring out how to use that advantage without endangering the women. "When we're there, we improvise."

Scaling a rock wall in the dark limited the number of weapons he could carry. There was the Glock in his shoulder holster, four clips of ammunition in his pockets and the Beretta in an ankle holster. That would have to be enough.

With Jack following, he moved swiftly through the forest. He had to reach Melinda before time ran out. He dug his toe into a crevice in the rock and started to climb.

THROUGHOUT HER LIFE, Melinda had tried to see the good in people. There had to be some shred of decency in Harlan. Hadn't he responded when she claimed to be in pain? Wasn't he a lawman for most of his life?

She sat up on the mattress with both hands resting protectively on her belly. Looking into his eyes, she saw an opaque blankness as though the lights had gone out. Still, she made her appeal. "You don't want to hurt me," she said. "Or my baby."

"Given the self-healing ability I assume you have, it's not possible for you to be injured."

"You took care of Drew for eight years." Harlan had served Drew up for experiments, and she despised him for that. But she tried to be sympathetic. "You protected him. Made sure he wasn't locked up in a cage. You gave him a healthy life."

"And look how he repaid me. Instead of cooperating, he ran. When he turned eighteen, he would have been out of the foster care system. Nobody would have kept track of him."

That must have been the plan all along. To wait until Drew was officially an adult and then to hand him over to Sykes. Apparently, Drew had escaped by a hairsbreadth. "You must have been angry when he left."

"He ruined everything. Your precious Drew destroyed everything I'd worked for and waited for."

"Were you supposed to receive a big payoff?"

"How many times do I have to tell you? It's not about the money." His expression darkened. "When Drew turned eighteen, I should have gotten my family back."

"Your family?" Drew hadn't mentioned anyone but Harlan and his wife.

"Belle and I had children. Identical triplet sons. We couldn't tell them apart unless we dressed them in different colors."

She made the connection. "Red, blue and green."

"Strong, healthy boys. Because of my FBI work, I knew from the start that they had the genetic traits that Sykes was looking for. I wanted them to be in his experiments, wanted them to be extraordinary. I gave my boys to Sykes and moved to South Dakota so I could be close to The Facility. In exchange, I was supposed to raise Drew."

She heard the bitterness in his voice. "It didn't turn out the way you expected."

"My boys never developed remarkable talents. But Drew became self-healing. His skill has a multitude of applications. He's a marketable commodity."

She prompted, "When he turned eighteen, what was supposed to happen?"

"Drew would go into The Facility. My boys would come home."

"Sykes wouldn't release your children."

"Worse," Harlan said. "They didn't want to be with me and Belle, didn't want to leave Sykes. They had a telepathic connection to him. I told Belle that I'd convince them to leave, that I'd bring our boys home. But she couldn't stand being separated from them. She killed herself."

"I'm sorry," she said.

His mouth twisted in a snarl. His eyes glittered with insane rage. He raised his gun hand and pointed the weapon at her. "I'll show Drew what it means to lose the woman he loves."

Struggling to keep the fear from her voice, she said, "If you kill me, you'll kill the baby. A valuable commodity."

"She's right," Blue said. He stepped around his father and grabbed her arm. "Come with me. I want the combination."

She had no choice but to stumble after him into the storage room. The booby-trapped safe was her only chance. "The combination is one-two-three."

"Ha!" Blue threw back his head. "That's stupid."

"Go ahead," she urged. "Try it. You'll hear the click and the safe will open."

He knelt in front of the safe and spun the dial. She tried to ease away from him, to put distance between herself and the bomb. How far did she have to go?

"Stop," Harlan ordered. He spoke loudly over the whir of the generator. "It's too easy. Drew must have set up some kind of booby trap."

Blue had already gone through the combination. "I heard a click."

"Don't open it." Harlan aimed the gun at her. "Let Melinda have that honor."

Her fear must have shown on her face, because his anger flared. He drew back his gun hand and smacked the side of her head. Pain exploded through her skull.

"Do it," Harlan ordered. "Open the damn thing."

She edged closer to the safe. "There's one more number."

She turned the lock to zero, took the handle and pulled. The safe opened.

Blue shoved her out of the way. He took out a canvas backpack and unzipped it. With a satisfied grin, he said, "Full of cash."

"Take it," Harlan said. "Now we get the hell out of here. Hold on to her."

Her hope of escape was dwindling fast. When Blue clasped her arm, she struggled. "I gave you the money. Let me go."

Harlan struck her again, this time in the arm. "I'm not supposed to injure you. Or use the device that induces blackout. But Sykes won't mind too much if I break your arm or your leg. I advise you to come along quietly."

When they came out of the storage room, they saw the door to the cabin standing open. Claudia was gone.

Melinda felt a swell of relief. Claudia was safe, thank goodness.

Harlan cursed and went to the surveillance cameras. He stared at the screens. "I don't see her. She must be huddled against the edge of the house. The cameras don't show that angle."

"I'll go after her," Blue said.

"She doesn't matter," Harlan said. "Jack's girl-friend doesn't have special abilities. If you see her, kill her."

"No," Melinda said. "You can't kill her in cold blood. Harlan, you were a federal agent, a lawman. You know the difference between right and wrong."

Harlan's chin jerked up. In profile, he had a certain nobility, and she hoped that she'd touched his sense of honor, reminding him of the ethics he once lived by.

"I've gone too far," he said. "I've got nothing to lose."

"Let's go," Blue said as he threw the backpack over his shoulder.

"You're right, son. Let's get the hell out of here."

Blue grabbed her around the waist and marched her toward the front door.

DREW HELD A GUN in each hand. Glock in the right. Beretta in the left. The next few seconds were crucial.

At least they'd rescued Claudia. Watching through the windows, Drew had seen Harlan and Melinda go into the storage room with Blue. He knew they couldn't hear well over the hum of the generator. That was when he and Jack made their move. Drew unlocked the door. Jack crept inside, scooped Claudia off the floor and brought her out here.

They could have made their stand against Harlan and Blue at that moment, but Drew didn't like the logistics. The storage room had no windows and no other access other than the one door. He didn't want Harlan and Blue barricaded in that small storage room with Melinda as a hostage.

Drew figured that Harlan would search for Claudia. Or, more likely, he'd send Blue. As soon as one or both of them stepped outside, Drew and Jack would attack.

Jack and Claudia hid on the right side of cabin. Drew had taken the opposite side. Whoever left the cabin—Blue or Harlan—would probably come in Drew's direction, which led to the road. And he'd be waiting.

They all came at once. Blue, Melinda and Harlan.

Blue was in front. Dressed all in black like a giant shadow, he held an automatic in his right hand. His left arm wrapped around Melinda's waist.

She was bleeding from a wound on her temple, but she didn't look scared. Her jaw was set. Her eyes blazed with anger as she struggled against his grasp.

Drew tried for a moment to get a shot at Blue. But he couldn't risk hitting Melinda by mistake. They were coming this way. He flattened his back against the exterior cabin wall and waited, hoping to time his attack for the right moment.

Using the element of surprise, he might be able to pry Melinda free from Blue's grasp before the big man was aware of what was happening.

Dealing with Harlan would be Jack's problem. Drew hoped the pre-cog was a good shot.

Blue came around the corner. Drew lunged. He tackled Blue around the midsection, yanking his gun hand down.

The three of them—Drew, Melinda and Blue— crashed to the ground. He heard shots being fired. Harlan screamed. Drew kept his focus on Blue. His grip on Melinda had loosened when he fell, and she fought her way free.

On the ground, he grappled with Blue. It was an uneven match. Blue had the advantage in weight and height, but Drew had motivation. His strength was multiplied tenfold. He had to win this fight. He had everything to live for.

He heard Jack yell, "Get away from him so I can get a shot."

Drew loosened his grip.

In an instant, Blue was on his feet. He ran without looking back, dodged behind Jack's SUV. He raised his gun.

Drew saw that Melinda was directly in his line of fire. He leaped in front of her. His only thought was to protect her and the baby.

A bullet burrowed into his chest. Hot lead. It felt like a molten poker stabbing through him. He lurched to his feet and returned fire.

Blue took off running. Clutching the strap of a backpack, he disappeared into the darkness of the surrounding forest.

Drew felt his knees buckle. He collapsed in the dirt.

ON THE MATTRESS where they'd made love, Melinda cradled Drew's head against her breast. He was unconscious. Though she felt his heart beating, his pulse grew weaker by the moment. She could feel him slipping away.

Claudia stood beside her. "Is there anything I can do?"

"The bleeding stopped," Melinda said. They'd taken off his jacket, holster and shirt. She'd washed his wound, but there was no need for a bandage. He wasn't bleeding externally. "I don't know what else to do. Regular first-aid procedures don't apply to Drew. He has to heal himself."

When Jack had carried him inside, Drew's breathing had been forced. She assumed his lung was pierced by the bullet. Now, he barely breathed at all. It was almost as though he'd given up the fight.

She squeezed his limp hand. *No, damn it, no. You can't die. Not now. Not ever.*

Jack pushed open the front door of the cabin and stalked inside. His expression showed discouragement.

Claudia went to him. "Did you catch Blue?"

"He made it to his vehicle and drove away." Jack came closer to the mattress. "How is he?"

"He'll make it."

With all her heart, she believed Drew would survive. He'd never been shot before, and she had no idea what kind of damage had been done to his internal organs. But she believed in his ability. His body would repair itself.

"I want to call for medical help," Jack said. "I need to inform the FBI that Harlan is dead."

"Promise me," Melinda said, "that he won't be given a hero's burial."

Harlan had betrayed everything he should have represented. He was worse than a common criminal, and she was glad that Jack had shot him when he came out of the cabin.

"Should I make the call?"

Drew wouldn't want the FBI to know the location of his cabin. Nor would he want to be treated by the medical establishment. But if they could help him…

A shudder went through his body. He exhaled a gasp.

She rested her hand against his chest. And felt nothing.

His heart had stopped.

It was over.

She held him tightly against her. Hot tears streaked down her cheeks. "I love you," she whispered. "Drew, you can't leave me. I love you."

Inside, she was cold and empty. How the hell could she go on living without him? He died protecting her and the baby. He'd given his life for her.

She stroked his forehead. His body was still warm. She pressed her lips against his for one last kiss.

He responded. *Am I dreaming?*

No, he was definitely kissing her back.

His eyelids opened. He whispered, "I love you, too."

She felt his pulse. It was strong. "Are you—"

"Not dead." His arm lifted and he touched the place on his bare chest where he'd been shot. "Not dead yet."

"Son of a bitch," Jack said. "You made it."

Drew nodded slowly. "Give us some privacy, okay?"

"You got it, buddy." Jack took Claudia's hand and led her toward the door. "Whatever you want."

When the door closed behind them, Drew looked into her eyes. "There's something I need to give you."

"It still hurts, doesn't it? The bullet wound."

"Oh, yeah."

She wiped the tears from her cheeks. "You should rest. You don't have to give me a god-damned thing."

His eyebrows raised. "You swore."

"I've been a little tense."

His grin was the most wonderful sight she'd ever seen. He dug into his jeans pocket and took out her Swiss Army watch. "I promised to bring this back to you."

"Thank you."

When she reached for it, he held the band. "It's not a ring, but I want it to mean something. As long as you have this watch, we have all the time in the world. Together."

She was crying again. This time, from happiness. "You and me. And the baby."

"Marry me, Melinda."

"Yes." She fastened the watch onto her wrist. For the rest of her life, she would live with this remarkable man. "Oh, golly, yes."

* * * * *

Don't miss the thrilling conclusion of
MAXIUM MEN *next month.*
Look for ENIGMA by award-winning
author Carla Cassidy wherever
Harlequin Intrigue books are sold!

Harlequin offers a romance for every mood!
See below for a sneak peek from
our paranormal romance line,
Silhouette® Nocturne™.
Enjoy a preview of REUNION by
USA TODAY bestselling author
Lindsay McKenna.

Aella closed her eyes and sensed a distinct shift, like movement from the world around her to the unseen world.

She opened her eyes. And had a slight shock at the man standing ten feet away. He wasn't just any man. Her heart leaped and pounded. He reminded her of a fierce warrior from an ancient civilization. Incan? She wasn't sure but she felt his deep power and masculinity.

I'm Aella. Are you the guardian of this sacred site? she asked, hoping her telepathy was strong.

Fox's entire body soared with joy. Fox struggled to put his personal pleasure aside.

Greetings, Aella. I'm the assistant guardian to

this sacred area. You may call me Fox. How can I be of service to you, Aella? he asked.

I'm searching for a green sphere. A legend says that the Emperor Pachacuti had seven emerald spheres created for the Emerald Key necklace. He had seven of his priestesses and priests travel the world to hide these spheres from evil forces. It is said that when all seven spheres are found, restrung and worn, that Light will return to the Earth. The fourth sphere is here, at your sacred site. Are you aware of it? Aella held her breath. She loved looking at him, especially his sensual mouth. The desire to kiss him came out of nowhere.

Fox was stunned by the request. *I know of the Emerald Key necklace because I served the emperor at the time it was created. However, I did not realize that one of the spheres is here.*

Aella felt sad. Why? Every time she looked at Fox, her heart felt as if it would tear out of her chest. *May I stay in touch with you as I work with this site?* she asked.

Of course. Fox wanted nothing more than to be here with her. To absorb her ephemeral beauty and hear her speak once more.

Aella's spirit lifted. What *was* this strange connection between them? Her curiosity was strong, but she had more pressing matters. In the next few days, Aella knew her life would change forever. How, she had no idea....

Look for REUNION by
USA TODAY *bestselling author*
Lindsay McKenna,
available April 2010,
only from Silhouette® Nocturne™.

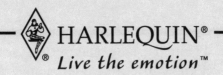

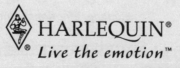

Harlequin® Historical
Historical Romantic Adventure!

Imagine a time of chivalrous knights and unconventional ladies, roguish rakes and impetuous heiresses, rugged cowboys and spirited frontierswomen— these rich and vivid tales will capture your imagination!

Harlequin Historical... they're too good to miss!

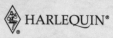

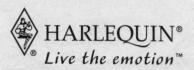

HARLEQUIN®

Super Romance®

…there's more to the story!

Superromance.
A *big* satisfying read about unforgettable
characters. Each month we offer *six* very different
stories that range from family drama to adventure
and mystery, from highly emotional stories to
romantic comedies—and much more! Stories
about people you'll believe in and care about.
Stories too compelling to put down.…

Our authors are among today's *best* romance
writers. You'll find familiar names and talented
newcomers. Many of them are award winners—
and you'll see why!

If you want the biggest and best
in romance fiction, you'll get it
from Superromance!

Exciting, Emotional, Unexpected…

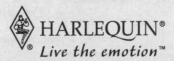

HARLEQUIN®
Live the emotion™

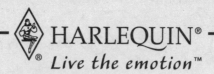